TALES OF THE MIRRORS

TALES OF THE MIRRORS

BOOK 1

FABLES

Peddar Panga

ISBN: 0692646558
ISBN 13: 9780692646557
Library of Congress Control Number: 2016904012
Peddar Panga , San Antonio, TEXAS

To Medard Mwanuke Panga,
for her love and support.

.

NOTE FROM THE AUTHOR

MY GRANDFATHER, KISHINDE Yumba Pikwa, and my father, Rev. Jean Claude Mpanga Lumbidji Mwana, are great storytellers. They always narrate their stories with love and great passion as if they are living the images presently happening on their inner screens. I call these two people my mirrors. When I look at them, I see my own reflection.

Curiously, my wife, Medard Mwanuke Panga, to whom I dedicate this book, is a great storyteller, too. She narrates her stories with great excitement, gestures, and changes in her voice tones, to name just those few qualities, as if she is part of the story she is telling.

The mirrors I'm referring to in the title of this book are my grandparents and parents, as well as the consciousness of each one of us, because consciousness is the great mirror of each individual. Consciousness tells you a story each time, whether you face a problem or not. And life rewards each one of us according to the tales of his or her consciousness. As Father always told me, "Each event of your life tells a story about where you stand with life." Tales of the mirrors are just stories that may happen to each one of us.

When I was growing up, my grandpa and my dad always told me stories of personified animals, with a lesson or moral behind each. Today, I've decided to share some of the stories (fables) with the world. I will be releasing more stories in the future. Those stories have helped shape my life, boost my imagination, and lead my choices and decisions. I hope they are going to work for you as they worked for me.

My grandparents and parents always repeated to me the message that love is the major lesson behind almost every story; that love is universal;

that humans think well with images; and that lessons are easily mastered when they are linked to a story, a parable, or an illustration.

Some of the big lessons from my "mirrors" are related to personal discipline, security, pursuit of happiness, mastery of fear, and love. My dad called them the basic goals to achieve daily. He advised me to work hard, to save more, and to do everything possible to be happy.

"In the heart of every story is love," my grandfather told me repeatedly. "Love is the foundation of life. Speak and act with love; read and write with love; choose and decide with love; and eat and lead your life responsibly and with plenty of love. Then you will realize that the weight of life will be very light for you to carry."

My father added, "Love is the core and the basis of every story I'm telling you. Please be disciplined and master fear and tensions because they prevent love from expressing itself clearly."

Stories don't have a time or a generation frame. Stories are suitable for kids and adults alike. Stories of great poets like Aesop and Jean de La Fontaine are still as valid today as they were centuries ago.

I invite you into the world of my grandfather and my father, because all the following stories are theirs. They didn't tell them to me only but also to you, the reader, and to the whole world. I'm just a channel, and I hope you enjoy them.

With Love, Joy, and Respect,

Peddar Panga

Contents

CHAPTER 1

THE WOLF AND THE ANTELOPE

The Wolf and the Antelope

A SATISFIED WOLF was enjoying his lunch after successfully hunting a bunny. He felt the need for a bathroom. "Oh, this belly of mine!" he complained regretfully, rubbing his belly. "Can't it wait for me to finish enjoying my food?"

However, the pressure was high and unbearable. It urged him to go ahead for his instant relief.

Not willing to mess his copious table, he walked a short distance away from his lunch. He relieved himself as fast as he could but was startled to find his precious treasure gone when he returned to where he left it.

Rubbing his eyes, at first he laughed at himself because he thought his mind and vision were playing a game with him.

Incredible but true, the reality was obvious. His lunch was missing.

"What?" he sputtered in rage, drooling with desire for revenge. "I'll catch you, thief. I know you should be around."

He squinted at his surroundings and saw an antelope nearby, masticating something.

"I've caught you, little fool!" he chanted triumphantly in his mind. "You'll pay for this, girl!"

Undetected, the wolf slowly approached Madam Antelope and grabbed her.

"Return my food and I'll spare your life," the predator warned hoarsely as if his voice were escaping from one side of his vocal folds.

Caught off guard, the antelope thought the wolf was asking her about the grass she was eating.

"Master," she said, shivering. "I can't throw up what I've eaten already."

"So, it was you?" inquired the wolf with satisfaction. "How dare you steal the lunch that I so dearly won?" he asked, his voice sounding so coarse; it was as if his rage amplified it.

"I didn't know that it was yours," said the poor antelope unreasoningly, fighting to catch the scarce breathing air that seemed to escape her nares. "I was just passing by, and I saw this food and started to eat. I beg your pardon."

"You couldn't have finished all my food in just less than the five minutes it took me to relieve myself. Where did you hide the rest?"

The antelope realized that the wolf was referring to something other than the grass she was eating.

"What food are you talking about, Master?" asked the poor antelope with a trembling voice.

"My food you said you stole."

"I didn't steal any food," replied the antelope courageously, with a quaver. "I'm not a carnivore, sir. You and I eat different types of foods."

"Don't tell me that, idiot," said the wolf, grinding his teeth, his voice getting coarser than ever. "You admitted that you stole it. Why is there blood on your mouth, all round your lips, if you claim not to be carnivore?"

Using her hand, the antelope wiped her mouth to assess the veracity of the wolf's statement. No blood came up. She did it again. Nothing.

Looking in another direction, the wolf saw a fox eating something. "That's my guy," he groaned to himself, "not this one."

"I'll let you go, scoundrel!" said the wolf to the lady antelope after scratching her face with his fangs. He also pinched his nose and maw. "Thank God that you're still alive. But, never attempt to steal anybody's property again. That's my free advice to you."

The wolf released the poor antelope. She ghastly ran for her life without looking behind her.

A couple of miles away, she found her peers. One of them asked her with a worried attitude, "What happened to your face?"

Another one asked her, "Why are you running loose like a scary lady who just saw the face of a devil?"

The lady antelope, still panting, jumped on them and beat both of them to near death. If it weren't for the rest of her peers, she could have killed them while seeking revenge for her unfortunate encounter with the wolf.

Moral: Sometimes, life meets you with misfortunes. Maybe because you were in the wrong place at the wrong time. Other times, those misfortunes may inspire you to make better choices, cautions, and decisions the next time. Life brings an equal number of problems and solutions, but maybe with different levels of intensity. There is no need to discharge your anger on your close ones.

THE CROW AND THE HAMSTER

Beware of your limitations; the weight of your life may get lighter and easier for you to carry.

Stifling a yawn, an amazed hamster looked out the window. Every morning, his hobby was to contemplate the singing crow perched on top of a house across from the hamster's cage.

"Oh! He flies great, that crow!" he repeatedly told himself in amazement.

Finally, instead of sitting lazily and powerlessly contemplating the crow, and instead of dreaming about flying every night and every day, the hamster decided to take a step further. He really wanted to fly like the amazing crow.

"What's the secret for flying?" the hamster asked the crow as he approached him.

"Well!" replied the crow after clearing his voice. "First, you need to believe that you can fly, and then you need to try to fly."

"I've got no wings to fly with, master," retorted the rodent, making extreme efforts not to cry with envy.

"Oh, oh, oh, friend!" said the crow, smiling broadly like Santa Claus. "Do not curse yourself. Once you put limitations on yourself, you won't succeed. I once didn't have wings, either. But I believed I could fly."

"And you flew?" asked the hamster in disbelief.

"Sure, and I flew."

"And the wings came?"

"Yes, and the wings came," the crow dryly assured him.

From the top of the house, ready to accomplish a dream of a lifetime, the hamster imagined and believed that he could fly. He felt the wing on his back and knew that he was ready…He jumped…The ground received him with a great impact.

The crow came to assess the damage, as the hamster stayed immobile for a while.

"Go away!" shouted the hamster with a furious and complaining tone. "You've done this to me."

The crow rejected the responsibility.

"Hell no!" said the crow. "You did this to yourself."

"You told me to believe and try," the hamster said in a subdued voice, blaming the crow.

"Where was your faculty of discrimination?" retorted the crow with a mocking tone. He added, "Besides, you're the one who came to me."

Poor hamster had multiple broken bones but survived the shock. He learned the hard way that in life, it's better to be aware of one's limitations.

Moral: No matter what your dreams are, and no matter what anybody else tells you, inwardly, discriminate against or prejudice any thought, deed, dream, etc. that may cause a certain damage to yourself.

What I call faculty of discrimination is similar to what psychologists call critical faculty, an inner tool that filter our dreams, actions, and choices- to name just a few- to fit our standards, our nature, and our limitations. Discrimination would mean to find what is better for us.

CHAPTER 3

THE FOX AND THE ROOSTER

A TIMID FOX was extremely afraid of a rooster because he thought that the crown at the rooster's head was a burning fire. Each time the fox saw the rooster, he ran away as fast as he could to save himself up from the burning fire.

After a long period, the timid fox mastered his fear and went to offer the rooster his friendship.

"Would you be my friend, please?" the fox asked, romancing the rooster with a honey tone. "You're so beautiful and lucky. Everybody talks about you. I'm one of your biggest fans and admirers."

Flattered, the rooster made an effort not to crack emotionally. He believed he heard the world highest compliment ever. Joy filled his heart. He best concealed his positive emotions stimulated by the fox's court, then only said, smiling broadly, "Sure!"

Even though the fox was still afraid of the rooster's fire and avoided getting closer to him, the two new friends got along very well.

One day, after getting better acquainted with the rooster, the fox asked, "Hey, friend, show me your secret, please!"

"What secret?"

"How do you keep the fire at the top of your head burning twenty-four hours a day?"

The rooster's beak dropped in amazement, and he asked disbelievingly, "A burning fire?"

"Yes, at the top of your head. There is a nonstop burning fire."

"Hell no!" the rooster objected vehemently, laughing. "It's just a crown—one aspect of my beauty and pride that the creator granted to me as a special gift. It ain't no fire."

The fox wouldn't believe it. For him, there was fire at the rooster's head. His friend was probably trying to delude him.

The rooster took his friend's hand and passed it on top of his head.

"Feel it, friend." He innocently reassured him, "It's not fire; it's just part of my body."

Indeed, there was no fire. Delighted, the fox's mission was accomplished. His fears were washed out. From that day on, foxes started to eat roosters.

Moral: Your killer may be a friend you share the same plate with. Also, beware of your friends; tell them fewer or none of your secrets, if any. Be slow when answering a question posed by a friend. Some friends' missions in life are to learn your weaknesses and secrets and destroy you afterward.

THE MONKEY AND THE ROOSTER

A MONKEY WAS honorifically appointed by God as a special prophet to grant wishes to those who asked one. A rooster came to him, requesting a special accommodation. He was not satisfied with his life.

"I can't build a bed like other birds," explained the rooster, looking down in an ashamed manner. "I sleep poorly, and I'm the most worthless of all the birds, mostly because I'm the main food for humans, and I can't fly." He stayed quiet for a while and left his request in suspense.

"If I understand you correctly," said the monkey, jotting on a piece of paper without raising his face to his interlocutor, "you want to fly like the other birds, right?"

"Yes," the rooster rapidly retorted, but he added with hesitation, "That's a second priority."

"Your first priority is—" asked God's special ambassador, lifting his eyes to look at the rooster and setting down his pen.

"Better sleep," replied the rooster with a quaver. "A nice bed, nice sheets, and nice covers."

Without hesitation, God's envoy said, "Granted!"

The rooster wanted to say something more, but the monkey hit his hammer on the table and shouted, "Next!"

When the rooster got back home, he found a nice bed and everything else that he had requested—a nice mattress, nice sheets, and you name it. He and all the hens enjoyed a good night's sleep. Their best rest ever.

The next morning, the rooster went on his errands as always. The following night, he could not go to sleep. His bed and each of his species' beds smelled, and they were full of droppings from the night before.

As the representative of the gallinacean family, the rooster saw a mob of his peers outside his door in the morning. "We couldn't go to sleep, and we can't wash our dirty sheets and beds," explained one of them.

The rooster rushed to see the wise monkey, praying for his grace once again.

"I'm sorry, Your Excellence!" stammered the rooster. He cleared his throat. "I think I and all my siblings need to be cured from defecating uncontrollably and continually. My nice bed is messed up and smelly. My brothers and I couldn't sleep last night."

"Sorry," retorted the monkey, raising his eyebrows and shrugging, "I have the power to grant only one wish to every requester." He paused to study the reaction of the rooster. "There is not much I can do anymore."

The rooster went back home, dejected with his head cast down and his wings loose as if they were heavy to carry. He explained to his fellows what the monkey had said.

"You should've thought about that before," one of them reproached the rooster.

"I told you about it, but you ignored me," another hen accused.

"Best sleep and beds weren't our priority," said regally a young hen. "We kept fighting for freedom, equality between hens and humans, but you chose the better sleep. Why did you choose a so low need?"

It was too late, and the ambassador rooster could not help. He just curved his back and looked on the floor. The hens missed a golden opportunity to change their fate because of his poor choice.

Moral: Know or set your priorities. Abraham Maslow established a hierarchy of needs. Fulfill your needs from the bottom up, like in a pyramid. Otherwise, you will pick an ant while what you needed was an elephant. An elephant will crush an ant, so make sure that the bigger animal is at the base of your pyramid.

CHAPTER 5

THE CHIMPANZEE AND THE PUMA

A CHIMPANZEE, LIVING at the border of a territory, used to wake up all the chimpanzees in the village at night. "Puma...puma...a puma is attacking...a puma is attacking us!" he constantly screamed.

Alerted, all the chimpanzees would wake up and grab knives, arrows, heavy wooden sticks, metals, and many other weapons, ready to defend themselves against the invader.

The chimpanzee caller would mock them with loud laughs.

"Eh! Eh! Eh!" uttered the tricky chimpanzee. "See how you all look like wet zombies? There is no puma around."

The mocking sessions continued for several nights. Each time, the chimpanzees would wake up to find the village empty except for the chimpanzee caller.

One night, a true puma invaded the village. Since the caller's cage was near the border, the puma attacked it first.

The chimpanzee caller screamed very loud and called for help, but no one came out to respond to his distress.

"I'm not joking tonight," the attacked chimpanzee cried out desperately. "The puma is really here, and he is about to devour me. Come, please. Come save me."

This particular call sounded so sincere to many of the villagers, because it was mixed with great emotions. However, no one came out. No one cared. The entire village knew about his ploys and games, and ignored him.

In the morning, the chimpanzees found blood and other remains of the chimpanzee caller, including his bones. The puma effectively ate him.

Morals:

1) When you act like a fool, who are you really mocking? Yourself!
2) When you lie repeatedly, people will not believe you even if you are telling the truth.

CHAPTER 6

PIG SENIOR AND PIG JUNIOR

PIG SENIOR'S FAMILY was the only troubled household on the farm.

Almost every day, Pig Junior nearly beat his hated father to death, to the bewilderment of almost everyone on the farm.

Friends of Pig Junior's decided to stop being inactive bystanders. They met to find the solution to their friend's unusual behavior. They all respected and loved their parents. They all acknowledged the lovely discipline and spankings they received from their parents as teaching techniques that parents use for the benefit of their children.

"Beating your own father?" said one of Pig Junior's friends, using peculiar hand gestures, during their conference. "I just don't understand. I don't even try to open my mouth when my father speaks to me..."

The speaker stopped short when one of Pig Senior's friends entered their meeting place. The unexpected presence of an uninvited adult stunned every participant.

"Hey, guys!" saluted the adult pig with authority. "I urge you not to worry. I grew up with Pig Senior. He used to beat the hell out of his father the same way he's getting beaten up by his own son. In my humble opinion, he's being paid back for what he did to his father."

The conference attendees were shocked. Everybody's snout dropped in astonishment.

The old pig added, "Life teaches better than any professor. Life makes you face your deeds and pay for them with a true coin. One day, your friend Pig Junior will have to pay back what he's doing to his father now. It just goes in circles."

The conference attendees agreed about life's payback rule but decided to intervene if their friend Pig Junior attempted to attack his father again.

Moral: Beware of what you sow today because you will have to reap it sooner or later.

CHAPTER 7

A RAT AND MANGOES

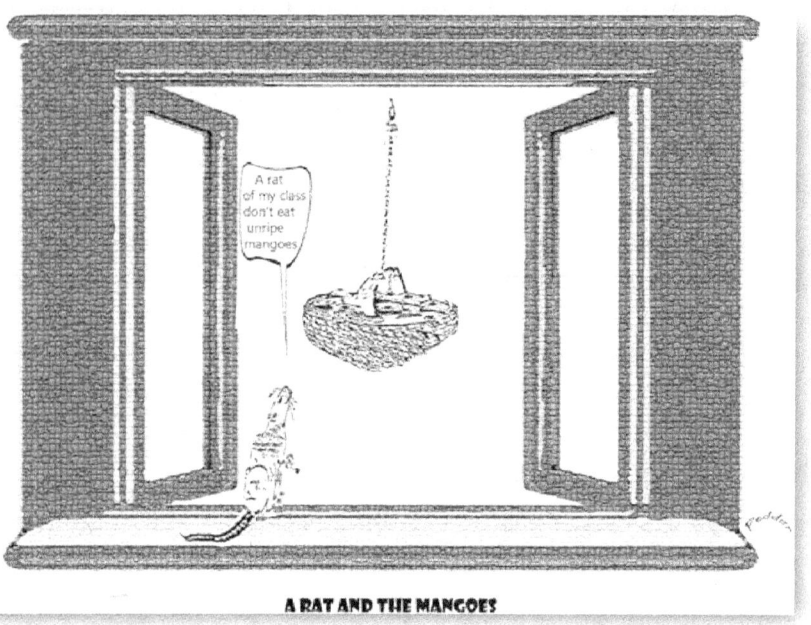

A RAT AND THE MANGOES

AN INNOCENT RAT came up by chance near a window where, nearby, a basket full of ripe mangoes was oscillating like a pendulum, suspended from the roof by a rope.

To get to the mangoes, the rat had either to jump from the window to the basket or to crawl around, reach the roof, then climb down the cord to the basket.

The rat attempted the crawls and the jumps, but he was unsuccessful. The mangoes' owner so precociously knew about rats that he placed his fruits out of their reach.

After several tries, the rat sputtered in despair, "I will leave those mangoes alone. They are not ripe. I don't need them. I don't eat unripe fruits."

Even though the delicious smell of the ripe mangoes was still inviting his senses, the rat gave up and minimized the fruits, a useful excuse to calm himself down.

Moral: Failed attempts turn desired items into deceiving and ugly ones. A gorgeous woman may be neglected and called ugly by a man after he had tried unsuccessfully to win her heart. It's one of the defense mechanisms: to find rational excuses over unpleasant events.

CHAPTER 8

THE DUCKS AND THE MOSQUITO

The Ducks and the Mosquito

A DUCK WENT to a pond. As soon as he started to swim, a mosquito approached him, courting him for friendship. "I'd like to be your friend, please!"

"Don't come closer," warned the duck calmly, not impressed at all by the mosquito's courtship. "You gotta stay away from me unless you wanna perish."

"You know what?" insisted the wooer, not willing to give up. "I'm a great singer—an apex celebrity. You won't be deceived in my company." He tried to play some good notes of music.

"Don't get closer!" ordered the duck after attempting to slap him. "I got malaria because of you."

"Because of me?"

"Yeah!" said the duck, his voice reaching a crescendo. "One of you guys bit me and made me sick."

"Why didn't you protect yourself?"

"He came to me with a sugary tone," the duck replied regretfully, shaking his head, "the same way that you are coming to me now. He made me sigh dreamily about his singing ability. I came to realize that he only wanted one thing: his food, my blood. As soon as he got what he wanted, he left as quickly as he came, but not without contaminating me."

"Sorry!" said the mosquito in diminuendo. "But I'm not like my brothers. Everybody's different. I'm really a good guy, and I'm willing to be your friend. You won't be deceived. Besides, I may fix what others messed on you."

"Negative!" objected the duck, shaking his wings. "You are all the same. Bite me once, not twice. I got smart already."

"Please!" insisted the mosquito, not willing to give up.

"No!" the duck categorically refused. "Why did you come to me, anyway? Don't you have other friends?"

The duck's big brother arrived and immediately intervened. He chased the mosquito away, freeing his brother from continued harassment.

"Congratulation, brother," said the arriving duck, "you did a good job on defending yourself."

"Thank you."

"Honestly," explained the duck's brother with an attitude of someone who knows, "your blood smells good to any mosquito's nose. If you don't protect yourself against them, they gotta come to you, singing harmfully to your ears, not only to thank you for your invitation for them to bite you, but also for your stupidity in being vulnerable by choice." He sighed. "Same goes with all parasites. There are millions of them around us. They mostly come to us by invitation. So, protecting yourself is the key to keeping them away from you."

"How can I protect better myself?" asked the younger brother. "At least I said no and backed away."

"You went to the mosquito," said the big brother. "You approached its habitat. It got an opportunity to attempt to bite you. This pond is unsafe; it is full of mosquitos and should be off-limits. The closer you get to it, the more exposed to trouble you get. The more you approach dangerous places, the less your personal protection becomes." He stopped.

"Go ahead."

"We gotta get out of here," concluded the big brother duck, with a commanding tone, "now!"

Moral: To be cautious and avoid everything that may cause harm, including some places, peoples, and behaviors, is one of better defenses against any threat or trouble that may come your way. That's personal security. It's part of personal discipline.

CHAPTER 9

THE BONOBOS AND THE OCELOT

A BONOBO SINGLE mother loved her unique son a lot. The son was a "teenager" bonobo, trying to live his life free of parental supervision.

During his rebellious times, the teen bonobo would act almost exactly against his mother's directions. When his mother, for example, would tell him to avoid some of his friends whom she judged to have bad influences, the son would not care, and he kept acting against her mother's orders.

The mother's chief concern was her son's safety. She loved him to such extent that her son's misconducts hurt her deeply. The later would come late at night, drunk and smelling strongly of marijuana. In addition, he didn't like the reaction of his mother.

"Don't put handcuffs on my freedom, Mama," objected the son bonobo, waving his hands in front of his chest in opposite directions, on a particular night. "I'm a grown-up bonobo."

"Coming back home late and intoxicated is not freedom," explained the mother, greatly worried. "It's irresponsibility." She looked into his eyes. "The friends you are following don't love you. They are controlling you. They are using you against yourself. None of your friends will be around when you get in trouble." She took a deep breath. "You think yourself to be enjoying the time of your youth, but in reality, you are destroying yourself. None of your friends love you. Someone who loves and cares about you will be concerned about your conduct. He will not acclaim, applaud, and approve you when you get late home at night. I can't allow you to go out anymore. Do you understand?"

"Mama," protested the son bonobo, "you're so embarrassing. You never gave me peace, but only drama and a hard time. I'm tired. I wanna live my life the way I want it, with no restriction and no evil-watching eye like you."

"No, son," explained the mother, with a pinched face clearly expressing lines of concern. "Our society is governed by rules and regulations. You can't cross every limit and walk free. You will face charges. As for me, I can't quite stand watching you mess up your life. I gotta intervene. Just help me, son. I may get a heart attack because of you. It happens that every time you go out, I stay awake, praying and very worried about you. So, you're not going out anymore starting today, understood?"

The son cared the least in the world. He ignored his mother's mandates and kept the same routine almost every night. Yet his mother never got tired of reproaching him.

The situation escalated one day when the bonobo son failed to tolerate his mother's reprimands.

"I've had enough, Mama," the son bonobo yelled. "You're the worst mother in the world. And I will tell you the truth: if it had happened that you were born later than the time of your birth, I could have married you."

Mother Bonobo's body reacted in a surprise mode. She automatically slapped him. Then bitter tears dropped from her face.

The son rubbed his cheek and said, "Starting today, you're no longer my mother. Not anymore."

"You're no longer my son anymore, either," retorted the mother, her lips trembling with rage. "I shouldn't have brought you to the world. How dare you to tell me that you could have married me if I were of your generation? How dare you, son?"

It mattered little to the son bonobo. He waved his hand, by his head, from front to back, in a sign meaning Go Away. He left his mother and went to live with his peers.

Days passed.

One particular day, an ocelot attacked the bonobo village. Everybody, under great panic, was running amuck to save his life. The invader needed only one target, and it had already found one. It was the Bonobo Son.

The ocelot chased him and him only. The son bonobo screamed for help, but all ignored his distress calls.

Mother Bonobo, from her hiding place, heard and concluded that the voice of the SOS caller was her son's. She courageously grabbed a piece of wood and went to save him, to the extreme bewilderments of the villagers.

The son was running in the direction his mother was coming from.

Mother Bonobo ran with rage and powerfully hit the mighty attacking ocelot with the wood. The impact was so strong that invader died on the spot.

Everything seemed to come to a standstill. The son bonobo stopped to run and scream. And a dead silence covered the village, during which Mother Bonobo kept holding her weapon, ready to strike the ocelot again.

After the moment of suspense, the entire village approached the scene. It was incredible but true. A bonobo lady, fueled by the love for her son, had just killed a mighty ocelot with a piece of wood, to save her son from the danger.

The son bonobo, crying, hugged his mother with great passion. Never before he has ever felt so loved.

"Thank you, Mama!" said he, with great emotion. "And I'm sorry for every wrong that I said to you. I'm always your son, and everybody here has witnessed how much you love me. You are and you will be always my mother. Even in a future life, if any, please, be always my mother."

"I love you too, son!" said Mother Bonobo, with a trembling voice filled with great sensation.

A soft breeze passed by, making tree leaves play soft music similar to that of a flute. Trees bowed their heads to pay their respect to the event.

The entire village applauded. Other villagers felt the strong bond of love between mother and son, so they cried of love, too. Love fueled the mother to save her son. It was also probably love that increased the striking power of the mother's blow to the ocelot. It was again love that pushed the mother to forget about any problem that existed between the two. Love forgives.

Moral: Love is amazing…Love is capable of producing miracles.

CHAPTER 10

FATHER DEER AND SON

AFTER FACING A drought and a lack of food in their territory, Father Deer took his son on an adventure in search of food. After a long walk, they found a gigantic green farm with fresh and abundant crops. The two explorers collected enough food for themselves and for their family. They expected the provisions to last for weeks.

Back home, Father Deer said to his son, "Never attempt to return to the farm we just left. In the case that we need more food, we will have to go search somewhere else. Do you understand?"

Bowing, the son said, "Yes, Dad! I won't return." But he added, posing a question, "Why not, Dad? We still need a lot of food for our survival. The drought—nobody knows how long it's gonna last. The farm we found was a blessing for us."

"We did steal," the father deer affirmed calmly. "The farm and the crops aren't ours. The farm owner may set traps to prevent future breaches. A similar scenario happened to one of your uncles, my brother. You didn't know him because he died before you were born. He was trapped in a snare after he returned to a farm he had gone to the day before. We don't need such an event to happen again in our family."

Son Deer assured his father that he wouldn't return to the farm in question. However, at night, he thought, "I'll go back to that farm as early as I can. I'll bring enough food for the benefit of the whole family. Even Dad knows that I'm the luckiest being on earth and nothing can hurt me. Doom always hurts others, not me. I'm immune from danger. I'm cautious, too. I can't fall into anybody's trap. If my uncle fell into a trap, it doesn't mean that I've got to fall into a trap, too. Moreover, the farm owner mightn't be aware of the damage we've done to his crops. Therefore, going as early as I can will be wise. I gotta go."

The son deer left for the farm as early as he could. He made it to the farm, but he didn't make it back home.

At noon, Father Deer remarked on the absence of his son. "Where is my son?" he inquired with great concern. Nobody knew. He was nowhere to be found. Father Deer, by experience, guessed where his son could be found. He only prayed that nothing unpleasant met him.

He went back to the farm they had visited the day before. He found his son there caught in a trap. Fortunately, he rescued him before the farm owner found him.

Morals:

1) Kids, please listen to your parents. They speak from experience. They saw and knew a lot of things before you were born.

2) When you return to a "negative" action that you escaped un-harmed, chances are that you will get caught.

3) Many believe themselves to be immune from dangers. They act with the conviction that inconvenience only happens to others, not to them. That naïve belief can't help but precipitate their eventual downfall.

4) You don't need to learn all of life's lessons by yourself. Let history, observation, and experienced people help you learn from the voices of experience and wisdom.

CHAPTER 11

THE LAMB AND THE CROCODILE

A WOUNDED LAMB was walking slowly, carefully dragging his disabled foot as he tried to join his flock. He reached a riverbank but didn't have any idea how to cross it. He sat powerlessly and desperately hoped for a miracle to happen.

Squinting at his surroundings, the lamb saw a shape lying on the sand of the river. At first he thought that it was just a mirage, but he courageously walked toward it.

"I'm lucky!" whispered the lamb. It was a crocodile taking a nap. "You think about help, and it comes your way from heaven," the lamb concluded joyfully, thanking divine providence for such a golden hand.

Unaware of the danger of his frantic action, the lamb woke the crocodile up.

The mighty being had been dreaming of a dessert after a very huge lunch. He stammered some unintelligible words, cursing against whoever disturbed his sugary respite.

After rubbing his eyes, the mighty crocodile could not believe it. He was surprised to see a fresh, babyish lamb standing in front of him. "You dream of a dessert," he thought, "and it comes to you by itself, with no effort on your part." However, sleepy as he was, he concluded to that his mind was playing a trick on him. So he went back to sleep.

The lamb, shaking the crocodile again, said with a baby-like, soft tone, "Master Crocodile, I need your help extremely."

Mighty crocodile finally woke up. He rubbed his eyes once again to wipe off his sleep. He could not believe the reality offered in front of him. A lamb was effectively there, begging him to be eaten. Because the lamb looked so innocent, the crocodile mastered his impulse to jump at him and devour him without due process.

"How can I help you?" asked the reptile kindly, making an effort to make his voice sound lower and sweeter.

"I need to cross the river, please," the lamb said sweetly, with a voice able to seduce an angel. "My family crossed the river earlier, and I can't swim because of my wounded foot."

"Sure! I can do that!" the crocodile agreed with a smile. He scornfully nodded, finally finding a reason to have the immature lamb as food. "What you need to do is ride on my back. I will help you cross the river."

The lamb hurriedly jumped on the reptile's back. The crocodile swam across the river and dropped the lamb on the other side. The innocent lamb graciously thanked him and started to walk off.

"Hold on, baby!" ordered the crocodile after holding the lamb on his foot. His voice sounded more frightening than ever. "You can't just walk away like that. You owe me."

Startled, the lamb blushed and said, "Master, I asked you for help. There was no agreement between us that I would pay you."

"Hell no," the mighty crocodile objected brutally with a deep, hoarse voice, but he smiled sarcastically. "Things don't work that way here. You have to pay with a true coin for every service that you receive, baby!"

"Nobody told me that, Master!" the lamb retorted fearfully, shivering. "How could I know?"

"Ignorance is not an excuse," the awful reptile insisted. "There's no apology, but only responsibility, when the service is already consumed. You gotta repair the damage."

"I don't have money, Master!" the lamb said forcibly, shaking.

"Then you gotta pay with your blood, boy!"

"Please, Master!" the lamb pleaded courageously. "If you allow me enough time, I will come back as soon as possible to pay you back with a true coin."

"Things don't work that way here, boy," the crocodile repeated rudely. "You don't pay a credit with a credit. There is no leeway, no layover, no pardon, and no delay once the due time has come."

The lamb tried to open his mouth but didn't succeed. The mighty crocodile jumped on him and devoured him with no more trial. He just thanked God for the self-brought dessert.

Moral: When asking a devil for help, expect to pay a hard price, even when you are ignorant.

CHAPTER 12

THE COW AND THE DEVIL

A SPECIAL COW spent his lifetime as an advocate of peace for humanity. After a successful career, he was granted an audience with a devil as a privilege and an honor for his hard advocacy work and for his accomplishments in life.

"Tell me, please, Your Majesty," said the cow with respect in the underworld palace. "I thought I would find chaos and destruction in your dwelling palace. But everything looks great, organized, and perfect." He paused to squint at his surroundings, and then asked, "Tell me, why you spread wars, miseries, destruction, and numerous ills into the universe?"

The king of the underworld made an effort to stifle a shriek of laughter. "Before I answer your question," said the devil, half smiling, "I'd like to ask you a question. Why is it that you cows help mankind so greatly?"

The cow wanted to answer, but the devil continued, "Why do you provide food, milk, transportation, worship, and so on to humans?"

"That's how we were designed by God," retorted the cow with a high pitch and a reassuring tone. "He gave us a mission to be of great help to humanity."

"Congratulation!" said the devil with triumph, smiling. "You are accomplishing your duties well. As for your concerns about me spreading calamities all around, it's part of my responsibilities. Many come to me and serve my purpose. They serve me but, instead of rewarding the, I severely punish them. Still all accuse me of being the source of –"

"People say you incite them to start all negative acts," interrupted the cow, with confidence. "You never got tired with your attacks, invasions and temptations. You use many ways and stratagems to lure people into your path."

"Yes, and I do achieve my duties perfectly," admitted the devil. "However, it's the duty of every being to kick me off his way and to triumph over every temptation as Job, in the Christian Bible and Jesus, after his frothy days fasting, are reported to have achieved."

The cow adjusted himself and wanted to say something but the underworld monarch continued, "Fear and illusion are ones of my biggest snares. I seeds up fear in each being to impress upon him his own negativity and inability to excel. I also plant fear and veils of illusions in every being, ones of my efficient tricks. If a being is worthy enough to be a being, he has to go beyond my circle of influence. Those who fail to push me out of their ways, and those who serve me faithfully, do it at their own expense. I don't reward them. I only use them, then mock them up, and finally I severely punish them for serving me and for being dumb enough to be my toys." He cleared his throat. "I'm just doing my jobs very well."

After the audience, the special cow left the underworld palace in bewilderment. He had a hard time buying the devil's statements.

Morals: Fulfill well your duties…

CHAPTER 13

THE COYOTE AND THE RAT

A COYOTE'S WIFE got pregnant. She had an irresistible craving for living rats only.

For the happiness of his wife, hubby coyote went on a hunting rampage, looking for rats everywhere. He did a good job providing a daily dinner for his lovely wife.

Almost every rat, once captured, felt powerless against the grabbing power of the massive coyote. Rats were taken without words like lambs to a slaughterhouse.

The hunting spree was so successful that the hunter coyote's confidence grew. The entire wilderness was alerted. Daily news spoke of him. Rodents spread the news and warnings about him to all rats, and his reputation grew.

One day, the famous hunter captured a talkative rat. On the way to the coyote's den, the rat struggled to release himself from his grasp, but the coyote was so extremely powerful that it looked like a newborn challenging a wrestling champion.

"If I can't use my strength," the loquacious rat thought with delight, "I can use my brain and my mouth to save myself."

The rat said to his abductor, "I need to use the bathroom. You know, I ate a lot of food, and my belly is full of dirt. I don't think your wife will be pleased with me as a meal if I'm smelly."

The coyote replied calmly with a very deep voice, "I have heard that before."

However, the rat could not give up. He said, "What if I give you my daughter instead? She's young, softer, and tender. Your wife will like her better than me."

No answer.

The rat talked and kept talking, using all kinds of rhetoric. He used excuses and explanations to convince the coyote to release him, but all the coyote did was to ignore him.

Finally, when they got to the coyote's den, the wife coyote could not wait. She was starving and grateful to her husband for the dinner.

"My final hour!" thought the rat in despair. "There's nobody here to deliver me. I've got to deliver myself, though," he concluded.

As the wife was ready to accept her present, the talkative rat said to the husband, "Wait a minute! Your wife is not even pregnant. She's fooling you because she is lazy. No pregnant coyote looks like her."

Those words did ring a bell in the hunter's brain. He had suspected the same thing before. He approached his wife with an inquiring look, softening his grab on the rat.

The rat took advantage of the situation, released himself from the coyote's clutches, and ran as fast as he could, not even attempting to look back.

After a long run, and after making sure that he was safe, the rat stopped, sighed, and exclaimed loudly, "Who can save you if not yourself?"

Moral: No matter how desperate your situation is, no matter how slim your chances of success are, try repeatedly. Your life and survival mostly depend, first, on you and on your creativity.

CHAPTER 14

MOTHER BEAR AND SON

Can you pay back the love of your parents with a true coin? A newlywed bear dared to try it.

The bear's mother came to visit the happy couple two weeks after her son's successful wedding ceremony.

At first, they lived together peacefully, but a quarrel between the wife bear and her mother-in-law soon turned their happy home into a pond of fire.

The son bear backed his wife and asked his mother to leave for the sake of his household.

"How could you do this to me, son?" complained the mother bear, really hurt by her son's decision. "You have no idea how much it cost me to raise you. For instance, when you were a baby, you cried inconsolably every night, all night long, and I stayed up all night for your benefit. I never got tired of raising you until you were able to live on your own. But now, for just a minor misunderstanding, you're getting tired of me already and asking me to leave?"

She paused to see her son's reaction.

"Now," she continued, looking straight into her son's eyes, "tell me, son. For just a dispute that even kids can solve, are you asking me to leave?"

"You know what, Mama?" replied the son bear without reasoning. "Weigh everything that you spent for me, even your love, and I'll pay you back. All I want is peace and happiness in my home. You happen to be the true obstacle to my household's joy." He paused, then added, "How much do you want so you can leave?"

Dumbstruck, the mother bear could not believe her ears. She stood quiet for a while, not knowing which decision to make—whether to leave or to stay there regardless of her son's wishes.

A bright idea crossed her mind.

"Well said, son," she whispered with confidence, a bright smile crossing her face. "I wanna get out of your house as soon as I can. But, since you wanna pay my love back, just do me a favor, please."

"Go ahead," said the son bear while his wife, standing behind him, was rubbing his shoulders.

"Leave me alone for one minute only, please. Then come back in this living room. You'll find the price of my love to you. Pay it before I leave your house."

The mother bear had diarrhea. As soon as her son and his wife left, she emptied her stomach in the living room.

A minute later, the couple returned to the living room.

"What have you done, Mama?" inquired the son bear, in disbelief, as he and his wife held their noses. "Have you lost your mind or what? There's a bathroom in this house. Why did you do it in the living room?"

"Oh, nothing!" the mother bear answered calmly. "What you have to do is just clean the mess as your repayment for everything I did for you as you requested." She started to walk out.

"Besides," added the mother, not the least bit worried, "that's not even one percent yet. You asked me to put a price on my love for you, right? You still owe me ninety-nine percent of everything I've done for you."

The poor bear son dropped on his knees. He knew his mother cleaned his poops multiple times, now his mother was asking him to clean her feces. He couldn't imagine cleaning up after her to repay her love to him. He had no other choice than to ask for forgiveness.

"I beg your pardon, Mama," he prayed, tears running down his face. "I didn't know that what I said was foolish. I'm always your son. Excuse me."

After a long litany, the mother finally accepted her son's apologies, but still required him and his wife to clean her wet discharge in the living room before she could effectively pardon them. "That way, you will learn to manage your tongue and anger as a fulltime job anytime you wanna react," added Mother Bear with a triumphing attitude.

They obeyed. However, as they were about to execute her command, she told them to stop. She hired cleaning professionals to clean up of the mess.

Moral: We owe a lot to our parents, even for the simple fact that they brought us to life in this world. Challenging them and thinking about repaying their love may not be a good idea. It may be worthless and senseless.

CHAPTER 15

A GOAT MOTHER OF TWO

A SINGLE GOAT mother of two sons liked the elder more than the younger. She gave to the elder more love, more advantages, more care, more attention, and everything else. She didn't care that her bias hurt the second son.

One day, while Mother Goat was away, the second son killed his big brother and dragged his body near a wolf den.

"Your brother is not around. Do you know where he is?" inquired the mother when she came back.

"A wolf came by and took him," said the young goat with a guilty tone and a trembling voice. "I hid."

Mother Goat was greatly distressed. She wept bitterly for days.

Her bias was responsible for planting the seeds of hatred into her baby son.

Moral: Favoritism generates all kinds of negative emotions, including jealousy, hostility, anger, envy, and hatred, to name just a few. It also brings war, destruction, and death among friends and families.

CHAPTER 16

UNCLE JAGUAR AND HIS NEPHEW

A BIG, SICK jaguar, unable to hunt, went to live with his sister, who was the mother of three little jaguars. She was a good hunter, and every morning, she left her den for her routine hunting job.

Out of habit, before she left the den, she would leave enough food for breakfast and lunch.

Her elder son took charge of sharing the food among his family members, but he always forgot to give a share to his uncle.

The big jaguar, sick he was, accepted his fate without a word. He would starve all day long and waited until the return of his sister before he could eat.

The situation continued for so long. One day, the big, sick jaguar had had enough. He secretly abducted the elder nephew and took him far from their territory.

"Today is your last day, boy!" announced the big jaguar coarsely. "I'm going to eat you." He paused when his nephew's eyes opened wide in surprise. "Say your last words," he added.

"What did I do, Uncle?" inquired the nephew, panting.

"You have been so greedy, little boy!" explained the big feline with a voice rougher than ever. "You never gave me my part of breakfast and lunch. It has been hurting me a lot, all along." He took a breath. "Now is your payback time." He took another breath. "Blame your death on yourself, on your actions, on your greediness."

Innocently, his little nephew, shivering, tried to explain. "My mommy never told me to give you the food. She just left the food to us as she did before you came to live with us. All this time I believed that she was leaving your part of the lunch to you and our part, the kids' share, to me." He lost his voice in the process. He cleared his throat and then continued, "Blame it on my mommy, not on me, please." His tone became more like a prayer, with a sweet, small, babyish voice. "I promise, Uncle! Starting today, I'll be giving you your share. Or, you'll be the one in charge of the distribution."

"It's too late, little boy!" emphasized the big feline. He had to clear his throat once more to soften his coarse voice.

"No!" the little jaguar screamed loudly as his uncle devoured him with no mercy.

Moral: Sharing even the most modest and insignificant things can spare us from unnecessary hatred, anger, and trouble.

CHAPTER 17

THE COBRA AND THE RABBIT

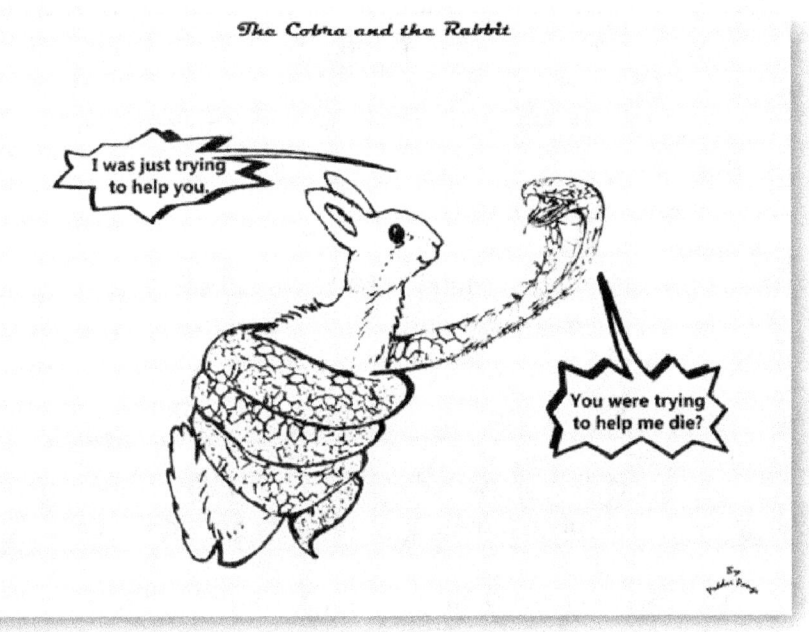

A HAPPY RABBIT was hiking around, looking for food. At one of her stops, she saw a mighty snake resting peacefully.

"I'm lucky!" thought the rabbit, her heart pounding. "If this evil creature was awake, it could probably had swallowed me today."

As she was about to continue her errands, she saw snots coming out of the mighty snake's nose.

"I can help wipe his nose," thought the rabbit blankly. "He's asleep and not a threat at all."

After a short hesitation, the rabbit found a leaf on the floor. She tried to help the resting reptile.

As soon as she was about to wipe the snake's nose, the dangerous serpent woke up, and, in a sudden move, grabbed her.

"What are you doing?" the snake asked intimidatingly, his eyes popping out as if they were bullets threatening to self-propel out of his eye sockets.

"I was just trying to help clean your nose," replied helplessly the rabbit, shaking with fear. She had to force her voice out, her neck being clutched by the legless creature.

"Wrong," argued the snake. "You were trying to kill me. And I'm wondering why."

"I can't kill you with a leaf!"

"Yes, you can. I saw you."

"No. I'm not strong enough to be able to kill you."

"If you were courageous enough to try to help me, as you said, then arguably you are strong enough to try to kill me."

"Please!" begged the rabbit. "I'm a mother of many. I don't wanna die."

"Likewise, lady!" emphasized the snake. "I didn't wanna die, either. What you don't want your neighbor to do to you, don't try to do it to him."

"I always wanted to be helped, and many have been helping me around. That's why I wanted to help you."

"You were trying to help me die?" argued the snake. "Now, what you tried to do to me, I'll do it to you."

The poor rabbit was defenseless as the mighty cobra constricted her first before biting her. The snake's poison killed her so fast.

"Sometimes generosity sucks!" the rabbit exclaimed regretfully before she expired.

"You invaded my space, lady," explained the snake to the dying rabbit. "I didn't invite you to clean my nose."

Moral: Sometimes, it happens that those you have helped or are trying to help will not be appreciative. They may not even recognize your good intents, especially if they didn't invite you to help them. So, beware of invading someone's personal space.

CHAPTER 18

THE LION, THE COUGAR, AND THE PANTHER

A LION, A cougar, and a panther tied a solid new friendship. All three were good hunters and agreed to share their food.

The first to honor their pact was the cougar. He brought into the group fresh prey he had just captured and divided it into three equal parts.

The great lion jumped on him, scratched his face, and injured him seriously. The panther intervened and proposed to divide the lunch in order to settle the fight.

The panther kept only the two legs of the prey: one for himself and one for the cougar. The remaining part of the prey he gave to the great lion.

"You really know how to divide," the lion congratulated him with satisfaction. "Where in the world did you learn to share correctly like this?"

The panther didn't say a word. He just shrugged.

"You merit a trophy for your wisdom," the lion added, nodding.

The panther finally said: "I know that some people like you have a natural right to receive more than ninety percent of a share."

Moral: It is said that all humans are born equal. Yet, there are some who would claim to have more rights than others. Thus, they demand a right to a larger part of a share. It may be just a greedy or a bully attitude; still, you may get in trouble, like the cougar did, if you try to share equally.

CHAPTER 19

THE HOUND AND THE FLY

The Hound and the Fly

If you got new wound, I will come back to you, I will kiss your behind and obey your orders.

If I don't have anything to give, you run away, right?

A SIMPLE GIVING habit may be enough to attract and control a friend. A naïve hound learned this the hard way when he met his former friend, the fly, after a long, unexplained separation.

"Hey, friend!" called the naïve hound with consternation and concern. "You used to come to me, along with your brothers, every single hour. My ears, full of wounds, were your favorite and resting spot. You ate and drank from them, and you followed me all around. But you suddenly disappeared without saying good-bye. Why?"

"My brothers and I," the fly answered unashamedly, "were your friends, and we followed you because you gave us all we needed, especially our food. There were interests involved." He rubbed his hands together. "Then, when your master cured your wounds, we needed new tables for our food and new friends who were able to satisfy us." He rubbed his hands again. "Sorry that we didn't say good-bye."

"What if my ears get new wounds?" asked the hound diligently. "You will come back again?"

"Absolutely!" the fly replied, and as per his natural habit, he rubbed his hands slightly. "We will kiss your behind; we will lick your feet; and we will bow at you and accomplish all your wills and commands."

Beginning that day, the hound learned that giving brings control.

Moral: To better exercise control, be the giver. Those who constantly receive from you will easily obey your orders.

CHAPTER 20

THE ROYAL HYENA GUARD

KING LION APPOINTED one of his favorite trustees, Lieutenant Hyena, to guard the eastern portion of his royal den.

To make his guardianship special, Lieutenant Hyena declared the portion under his surveillance as an off-limit sector. He had arrows, and he was ready to shoot everyone who would violate his ordinance.

As if an order attracts its opposite, as soon as he decreed his mandate, Lieutenant Hyena shot a passing violator.

"I made it clear," groaned the fierce guard as he approached the violator. "Don't you understand that you will die if you cross the boundaries of the king's palace?"

Checking the face of the victim, Lieutenant Hyena was dismayed to find that it was his father-in-law. He made emergency arrangements to save him. Fortunately, the hurt in-law recovered from his wound quickly after a short treatment.

The lieutenant vowed to be wise the next time before shooting his arrow at the trespassers.

Soon after, the elite guard forgot his vow. The hyena shot two intruders.

It was his sister and her lover lost in a dating adventure. His sister became permanently handicapped.

Lieutenant Hyena vowed to be even more cautious than before.

However, the desire to perfect his job outweighed his vows. Lieutenant Hyena didn't hesitate to shoot the next violator.

It was his mother, lost from a hunting experience. She died on the spot.

The excellent guard quit his job, judging himself unfit to perform it. The setting of the job and the way he was reacting to it didn't fit his ruffled nature. He was hurting himself emotionally, directly, in the line of his duties, by hurting his immediate family.

Moral: Be tolerant and relaxed before reacting. You may hurt yourself if you don't. Also, use discrimination, wisdom, and flexibility before decreeing and enforcing a rule, whether for yourself, at home, with family, or in the society. We live in the world surrounded by relatives and friends. We are called to support one another, not to destroy one another. Better give not much or less of yourself. Balance is the key.

CHAPTER 21

THE PANDA AND THE ALLIGATORS

The Panda and the Alligators

A PANDA OWED a hunter for saving his life. He promised the hunter that he would do anything that he would ask him in return for his favor. It happened that the hunter needed the heart of an alligator for multiple uses.

The panda, faithful to his word, went to look for an alligator on the bank of a river.

There was an alligator living near where the panda settled. He was sick, and no remedy given to him was sufficient to cure him. His doctor told him that the only remedy to cure his condition was for him to eat a panda's brain.

Coincidently, the sick alligator's brother went to look for a panda for his brain. He was surprised to meet one by the river. The panda was also surprised to have to make little effort to find his target."

"I'm lucky!" the panda exclaimed inwardly in joy. "You look for an alligator, and God sends you one."

Likewise, the alligator thought, "I'm lucky! You go search for a panda, and God grants your request right away."

He approached the panda.

"Hey, panda!" shouted the alligator with a thunderous voice that shook trees nearby. "I can do it the hard way or the easy way." He paused to assess the reaction of his adversary. "You can't escape from me. What I need is your brain only. Just give it to me, and I will spare you from more damage."

Panda needed the alligator's heart, too, but he felt powerless to attack the massive alligator—and suck his heart out of his chest—close to his dwelling place. Besides, the alligator had a couple of friends as backups.

The panda had a plan.

"You want my brain?" he asked with a broad smile. "It's easy to get it. But I left it about two miles away from here. If you can follow me, I'll give it to you for free."

The alligator looked behind him to assess his friends' approval. They acquiesced.

Panda's plan was to bring the alligators close to the hunters so they could finish them.

"Are you coming?" he asked with a heartening voice.

"Sure!" answered the alligator.

After two miles of walking, the panda pointed to a spot located about two miles away. "You see that tree over there?" he said with confidence. "That's where my brain is."

The alligator assented. But when they got to the tree, the panda pointed to another spot and another and another. No brain was ever found.

Finally, the alligators got exhausted. "Wait a minute!" said one of them. "You hide your brain so far from you?"

"Sure!" the panda assured him. "We're almost there."

Delighted, the alligator remarked, "I thought your brain was in your head."

"Eh! Eh! Eh!" The panda laughed wryly. "No panda keeps his brain in his head."

The alligators attacked the panda. He defended himself well, but he was outnumbered. He screamed for help. The hunter's village was not far away. The hunters came too late. Panda's brain was already sucked out of his head.

Moral: When fooling your peers, consider the time factor. The faster you fool, the sooner you escape. However, the longer you act, the more failure you attract.

CHAPTER 22

THE OLD MONKEY AND SONS

The Old Monkey and Sons

AFTER ENJOYING MORE than a hundred years of a healthy, productive, and happy life, an old monkey was approached by his three sons, who wanted to know the secret of his longevity.

"Be prudent like a cat and be as horribly sly as a snake," the wise old monkey said slowly with a rounding smile to his lips. After clearing his voice, he added, "You have one life alone. Give it the best you can. Protect it as the hen mother shields its baby chicks. Physically exercise often, take work as your best distraction, and love to the best of your ability, because love is the most important thing. Love is all you need."

To the old son, the old monkey said, "Avoid drinking alcohol and any other destructive habit like smoking and illegal drug abuse. That discipline will save you from multiple troubles against yourself and against your community."

Looking at the second son, the father monkey advised, "Avoid women and sex. They are sources of many troubles and deaths."

The wise monkey pulled the ears of his youngest son and said, "Money isn't bad if its serves you. Just don't let it control you. If you allow it to be your master, it'll hook you to power. Power destroys."

The three sons enjoyed his great advice and thanked their father for summarizing his wisdom about three vices: alcohol, women, and money. They went to carry on with their lives.

Many years later, the old monkey was dying. He inquired about the absence of his beloved sons. He was told that his elder son had been a drunkard who lacked the discipline to contain himself. He had gotten involved in a fight while intoxicated and was killed. The second son had loved women to the highest degree and contracted a sexually transmitted disease. Fortunately he got cured from it; yet, he died, killed by one of his lovers. The third son, the news said, was a successful businessperson, but money precipitated his death because of a conflict of power with another executive, and also because he used money as his power tool to satisfy all his animalistic needs and he lacked the discipline to control it.

The old, dying monkey held his head in his hands in despair. He cried for the loss of his sons. "Longevity is a fruit of self-love and self-discipline. Take advantage of it," he said to those at his bedside. "Buy my advice for your own protection; otherwise, you'll destroy your life at an early age as did my kids." Before he took his last breath, he added, "Change your mind, and you will control your world."

Moral: No matter how rich, fruitful, and self-explanatory the warnings are, if your mind, spirit, and conscience are not buying them, you may be a candidate for your own destruction.

CHAPTER 23

THE WOLVES AND THE FOX

A FOX WAS kidnapped by wolves and held prisoner in their turf. He became a slave and accomplished exhaustively every task he was forced to do with fewer breaks. Sometimes his workload was more than he could bear, but the wolves pushed him beyond his limits. Among his multiple tasks, the fox was unmercifully forced to carry, to push, or pull heavier loads than he could handle.

The fox's sufferings were so intense that he made every possible effort to free himself. Rebellion didn't work. In addition, every time he attempted to escape, the wolves caught him and imposed harsh penalties, such as lashings and waterboarding.

He constantly wrote to his brothers, the foxes, to request their help. All they could do was pay a ransom to free him. Nevertheless, his brothers, the foxes, seemed to have ignored his pleas.

After a long period that seemed like an eternity to the slave fox, to help himself adapt to his situation, he asked his conscience to adjust to his life's conditions. He forgot about being abused, used, and mistreated. He accepted the harsh direction of his life with joy.

The change didn't happen overnight. The fox had many ups and downs before he could accept and adapt to what he once called an unbearable life. He considered it a normal way of living, not as a harsh, punitive, or unlivable life. Working with no or fewer breaks became a normal way of living for him. He accomplished all his assigned task with no regret, and he found all works to be within his capacities.

It took a lengthy period before his brothers came to rescue him. They paid the fees required to free him, and the wolves released him on the spot. However, the freed hero refused to go with his brothers.

"No," argued the fox with a fierce resistance, "I'm loving my life now. I can't return to the way I used to live before I became a slave. It'll be very boring to me. I'm sure I'm not gonna make it. I wanna stay a slave, but stay busy for the remainder of my life."

"Why?" asked one of his brothers.

"Because I'm loving it. I've already adapted to this life, and I live it with no regret."

"Are you crazy or what?" protested one of his benefactors, not believing the freed fox. "You kept pummeling us with demands to free you up, didn't you? We spent years working hard and collecting enough for the exorbitant sum of money your jailers asked for your release. And that's the way you are repaying us for our labor?"

"Well," replied the slave fox, with a confident voice invoking mockery, "I really appreciate your help, but the situation has changed. I kept asking for your help then, but now I'm fine. I don't even recall if I was a free fox before I became a slave. So, I'm not going. I feel great now in my life."

The wolves had to intervene to settle the dispute. They told the stubborn fox that they couldn't keep him among them because he wasn't a slave anymore, nor was he a wolf. Then, and only then, the freed fox accepted his freedom and went with his brothers.

Years later, after his reeducation and settlement as a free fox within his herd, one of his brothers spoke to him with a serious manner.

"You know what, brother?" he said, with a tone of regret easily detectable in his voice. "The ransom we paid to free you from slavery wasn't enough. We only bought you partial freedom. I'm sorry that we kept that terrible secret from you. The truth is that we have to bring you back to the wolves again."

"Over my dead body!" the hero fox retorted shortly without even looking at his brother.

"I was just joking." His brother laughed very heartily for a long period. The rest of his family joined the joke and all had a good laugh about it.

The freed fox was again used to his life full of freedom and couldn't really imagine being a slave again. Adapting to his life circumstances, especially when he was a slave, was a temporary solution for the fox. He found no need to be a slave once again.

Moral: Life offers us the ability to adapt to our environment. Yet it's up us to make necessary choices and decisions and to work for the adaptation. If we believe that a specific life condition is hard and unbearable, it's going to be so. If we believe we can adapt, yes we will. Thus, life puts people in the perfect place for a specific time and for a specific life lesson. To survive, we need to adapt and learn from it.

CHAPTER 24

THE PARROT AND THE HORSES

A PARROT ACCEPTED an unusual position as a teacher for the horses. His boss, the farmer owner of the horses, chose him not only because he was talkative but also because of his generosity. The parrot was known to be among the great donors in that region.

Almost every day, Professor Parrot brought a gift to each of his students, the horses. He took advantage of his actions and transformed it as an element of control because the horses loved, adored, and obeyed him for of his giving habit.

One day, the parrot was completely devoid of resources. The time was so hard for him that he lacked the ability to provide his daily gifts for his student. All he had that day was just one carrot. How could he split it for twelve horses?

He just decided to give it to only one of them but which one to choose?

"Hey, guys," announced Professor Parrot with a sad tone. "I'm sorry. Today I've got nothing for y'all except the carrot I have in my hand. The luckiest of y'all will get it."

A huge silence followed and lasted only a few seconds.

"Who wants the carrot?" asked the teacher in higher tone.

All the horses but one jumped in excitement, each wanting the carrot to be given to him. There was competition of voices and gestures. Each horse needed the piece of food. And the fever to get chosen lasted a long while, during which some horses were on the verge of a fight.

Finally, Professor Parrot calmed the students and gave the carrot to the horse who stayed calm while others fought to win the nomination. Let's call him, Horse H.

"He showed a positive attitude," explained the parrot, to appease those who complained. "While you guys where excited, he was relaxed. He deserves it."

The next day, Professor Parrot, still devoid of resources, yet willing to give, brought only an apple to his class and he proceed the same way as he did the day before.

All the horses but Horse H stayed calm because they were advised the day before to practice relaxation. Horse H was the only one who showed relentlessness, and he won the sole gift of the day.

"He was excited today when y'all were calm," explained the parrot to the class because they complained harshly that he treated Horse H with favoritism. "Horse H showed a positive attitude, and great flexibility. He knows when to yield. He deserves the fruit."

Since all the class didn't agree with him, he added, "Use a positive attitude and be flexible with it according to the events around you. To be able to influence things around you, be calm and harmoniously relaxed when things are excited. But, when they are calm, try the best you can to fight to get what you need. In brief, know how to yield."

Moral: Attitude is part of wisdom. It is a fruit of spirit. Those who have a positive attitude and know to yield may influence events around them and conquer their destiny.

CHAPTER 25

THE CRAB AND THE ANTS

A WANDERING CRAB got a huge fruit that he intended to use as food for many days. However, he lived not far away from the ants' mound. He knew his neighbors' strong smelling and detection abilities. Thus, he planned to stay awake for twenty-four hours every day to protect his treasure from the ants' aggression until he had consumed it completely.

The crab knew that it was impossible to stay awake for twenty-four hours every day for days. So he came up with an idea: "Let me visit my friends, the ants. I've got a secret to tell them."

"Hey, friends!" the crab introduced himself after a warm reception from the ants. "Many of you don't know me, but I'm easy to get along with." He paused and made sure that the ants were following him with much attention. "When you get close to me and see me resting with my eyes closed, then, believe me, friends, I'm 100 percent awake. But, if you cross by my place and find me resting with my eyes open, it means that I'm profoundly sleeping. In that case, don't disturb me, please."

The ants believed him and thanked him for sharing his secret with them and for his kindness and sincerity.

At night, the ants detected and were attracted by the strong smell of a fruit. They tracked the smell and found its source to be the property of their friend crab. The latter was resting with his eyes closed.

The ant soldiers were ready to attack. However, their commander refused to allow them to go on their friend crab, but he promised them that he would order them to attack the next time. He explained that it was better to steal the fruit in secret than to risk the lives of many just for a morsel of food.

The ants left the crab alone but came back later. They found Mr. Crab resting up with his eyes open.

"Perfect timing!" shouted the commander of the expedition, smiling with satisfaction. He quickly gave order to his soldiers to quietly take the fruit. But the crab warded them off. He was awake.

Several other attempts to steal the fruit without bloodshed were unsuccessful. For several days, the crab was able to eat his treasured fruit alone and to enjoy his resting times.

Ultimately, the ants realized how the crab's plot fooled them. However, it was too late. The crab's food was resting in his belly.

Moral: Sometimes, life works like a game. The person who comes up with a plan for the game sets the rules and regulations. People will always fall into this game and play it according to the rules set. Curiously, even when the rules seem obviously fake and insane, there are millions of people who will believe and support them. Mass leaders use the game technique to control millions, usually for their own interests; they know that people will support them and allow them to have enough time to enjoy their "food."

CHAPTER 26

THE MERCHANT AND THE DEATH

A RICH MERCHANT got a chance to meet with an almighty entity known as Death. He didn't hesitate to ask the latter to grant him a wish.

"Go ahead," said Death with a thundering voice, nodding.

"Oh, Your Greatness!" started the merchant, cowering in a sign of respect. "I spent a lifetime investing to get to the level of wealth that I'm enjoying now. May I live for a thousand more years so I can enjoy my wealth to the fullest, please?"

"Granted!" Death said dryly without prevarication, to the merchant's disbelief. "However," added Death after a short silence, with a frown on

65

his face, "do not invite me to come to you because I won't be able to resist. If you avoid inviting me, then and only then you will enjoy your thousand years. Deal?"

"Deal!" the merchant agreed nonchalantly, with a glimmer of disbelief.

Death banged his fist on a table like a judge. "Pact sealed!"

The rich merchant thanked Death cordially as they parted.

Years passed.

One day, after drinking and driving irresponsibly, the rich merchant had a serious car accident. He found himself in serious condition. Then, Death came to take him.

"No way!" objected the merchant. "We have a pact to let me live longer than one thousand years."

"Sure!" agreed Death wryly, "But you were under strict orders to not invite me. By my nature, I'm very sensitive to invitations, and I respond very quickly."

"Give me another chance, please!" the merchant begged. "You didn't explain to me that an accident is an invitation."

Death granted him his request but emphatically warned him not to invite him anymore under any circumstance.

After several years, the merchant was involved in a gunfight. He was critically injured. Death didn't hesitate to come to pick him up.

"Not this time, please!" pleaded the rich merchant cordially. "I didn't formally invite you. Beside, I've got more than nine hundred years to go."

Indulgent as he was, Death understood him and gave him an extension. However, he warned him again to stay away from invitations.

More years passed. The rich merchant got sick after exposing himself to a toxic fume. His body became weak, gnawed by the sickness. It could not support life anymore.

"Get ready, friend!" announced Death when it came for him. "I'm taking you home."

"That will be in violation of your own pact with me," answered the merchant with confidence.

"You are the one who has violated the noninvitation clause of our pact," answered Death with determination and with more confidence than that of his interlocutor. "You've violated our pact several times by driving recklessly, by getting in a gunfight, and by exposing yourself to toxic fumes." He sighed. "This time, I won't budge. We gotta go."

Death took the resisting merchant, and that was it for him.

Moral: One "negative" act may mess up your entire life. Yet life offers many remedies to your choices and decisions, sparing you from unnecessary early ruin or death…At our birth, we sign a contract with life, but any negative action we take may be a way of inviting death to destroy us before our contract with life expires.

CHAPTER 27

THE ELEPHANT AND THE HARE

The Elephant and the Hare

PASSING BY, AN elephant trampled a baby hare, who died on the spot in front of his father.

To honor and avenge his daughter, the hare promised to publicly mock and dishonor the mighty elephant.

Seizing his courage into his hands, legs, and heart, the hare went to see the elephant.

"Eh, you elephant," the hare called out with confidence. "You've unmercifully crushed my daughter. I couldn't even bury her." The elephant ignored him. However, the hare added, "All the jungle will witness as I'll defeat you in a rope-pulling match."

Unable to express a mocking smile, the elephant's eyes opened wide—very wide—with a curious bewilderment. He stayed quiet for long seconds, laughed as loud as he could for long seconds, and then looked straight at the hare.

"What did you say?" asked the elephant, losing trust of his own ears.

"You killed my daughter in front of me," spoke the hare without flinching, pointing a finger at the giant he was challenging. "Her blood must be honored." He frowned, pointed his fist, and then hit it on his other hand. "I've already invited all the jungle to witness how I'll defeat you in rope pulling match tomorrow at noon."

The challenged elephant looked at the defying entity, then looked at his brothers in the herd.

"Hey, guys!" he called to the herd and said with a scornful tone. "Did you hear what this tiny creature just said?" The entire herd paid a listening ear. "He said he will defeat me in a rope-pulling challenge tomorrow at noon."

The rest of the herd of elephants laughed to an extreme level. Some nearly laughed to death, falling into comas or having heart attacks. Others laid on the ground, holding their chests, heads, and more. Still other elephants showed their incontinence: urine flowed uncontrollably from their bodies during their long, lengthy, and deep laughs.

Regaining his composure, and after sobering his face, the elephant rejected the challenge.

The hare insulted him and concluded that, "You're a coward, elephant. You're really a chicken."

The insults did produce a hurting effect on the elephant, and they made him change his mind. He finally accepted the challenge.

The next morning, the jungle stadium was full to bursting. All the jungle animals were in turmoil as they waited impatiently to witness the challenge of the century: the new-and-improved version of David versus Goliath. There were acclamations, endorsements, bids, and more.

At noon, the hare won the match after pulling the mighty elephant across a dividing line set as the victory line.

"You see how foolish you look now, biggie?" the hare yelled triumphantly to the defeated elephant. "This is a lesson that you should not underestimate anybody, and that you should respect every creature. Every being is important as much as you are no matter his size."

The defeated elephant returned quietly home, helped by his brothers, full of shame.

In reality, the hare didn't directly defeat the elephant as everybody in the jungle witnessed. The hippopotamus did.

The night before the challenge, the hare went to see the large animal and told him that the all jungle was set to witness the challenge issued to him by the elephant. The hippo accepted the challenge. The hare made enough arrangements to hide the hippo and the portion of the rope from himself, the hare, to the hippo. Everybody in the stadium saw only the elephant and the hare, but the latter was just in between the two giants.

Everybody, including the elephant, failed to recognize the true adversary of the "Goliath" because the hare used creativity, skills, and wisdom.

"Wisdom is greater than gigantism," the hare told himself with satisfaction.

Moral: Use your imagination, creativity, and skills to face challenges, especially when your own force is less useful.

CHAPTER 28

Two Hyenas

Two hyenas were great and inseparable friends. They grew up together and shared almost all of their belongings.

After the death of the king lion's right-hand man, the monarch appointed one of the two hyenas to fill the vacant prestigious position of royal aide-de-camp.

The appointed hyena became so busy with his duties that he could not see his friend as often. He just lacked time because the king's entire workload was under his supervision.

His greatest friend's visits became unwanted embarrassments. He finally gave orders to not welcome his friend to the royal palace anymore.

His friend complained, "Is that how you are treating me after all the time we spent together?"

The hyena royal aide-de-camp retorted vehemently: "I understand that we went through life together like Siamese twins. But that was then. Our lives at that time were tuned to the same music tone and to similar vibrations." He shook his head as a sign of regret. "Now we live in two completely different worlds with mismatched and opposite lifestyles. We can't play the same music, as our tune will sound awful and extremely discordant."

Moral: Indeed, success and/or new interests bring the separation of friends, of siblings, and of partners.

CHAPTER 29

THE BULL AND THE GIRAFFE

The Bull and the Giraffe

HUBBY BULL, A great worker and family provider, turned his wife, Giraffe, into a crazy, loving instrument. She bowed to him, washed his feet, kissed him all over, never gave him a hard time, and obeyed him like a slave.

"Your love will make me crazy!" the bull complained lovingly, one day, with a broad smile. Giraffe contented herself by laughing out loud in a sign of acquiescence.

After a work accident wherein Hubby Bull broke his legs, he became disabled, developed cancer afterward, and became unable to provide for the family.

His wife's general behaviors shifted from softness to hellishness. She became tense like a hot iron bar. She became talkative, impatient, impolite, and impossible to get along with. Yelling, rejecting, and insulting her hubby became a routine.

Finally, she had had enough and kicked the poor bull out of their household.

"Why are you doing this to me, wife?" the bull grumbled indignantly, trying to conceal his pain. He added, "After all I've done for you before my accident."

"Love and bounty go hand in hand," explained Madam Giraffe, unabashedly. "You can't have one and miss the other."

"Oh God!" prayed the bull. "Help each of your creatures to love one another unconditionally in happy and hard times with the same intensity, please."

Moral: The one who truly loves you is the one who shows his love not only during abundance but mostly during hard and scarce times.

CHAPTER 30

THE HEN AND THE ROACHES

IN A TERRITORY of roaches, Queen Hen was a powerful monarch. She reigned with extreme authority, as she was the only giant and different being in that country. She imposed a daily tax of nine roaches for her food—three each for her breakfast, lunch, and dinner. Her security was one of the best around. Very faithful roaches who executed her orders without questions guarded her. Those orders were carried out against their own brothers, the roaches.

One of Her Majesty's subjects, a mature roach, had only one lovely son that he securely hid from the faithful royal soldiers who abducted their brothers each day for the queen's food. However, royal intelligence services soon found out about the hidden son and took him to the palace—a perfect dinner for Her Majesty.

The old roach called an urgent meeting to raise the territory's awareness. He said, "Brethren, I've lost my dear son today. He may be eaten by the greedy queen anytime as she may end up eating each one of us and all our progeny." He paused. "Starting today, that queen ceases to be mine, and I need you to back me up. Decide that she's no longer your queen either, please. Because we're allowing her to exterminate us. If we don't stand, she'll continue to eat us, and we'll all be gone one day." Another pause. "She's alone, and even if she's protected by our brothers, they are all traitors. We're hundreds of thousands. If we stand together, we'll defeat her. What we need to do is just pack up our fears in a bag and ship them to unknown lands." He took a final pause before his conclusion. "Who will come with me? I gotta go now to save my son and all of us."

A huge uproar took effect. Many roaches feared for their lives. One of them said, "We understand you, old man. But did you assess the risk of your rebellion? Do you have logistics and plans for battle? Do you know what you mean?" He cleared his throat. "You can't just blindly engage in a disorderly adventure that's gonna cost thousands of lives and that has no guarantee of success. Insurrection means death. We may all die and not reach our goal. I'm scared. I'm sorry, I can't join."

Another uproar dominated the crowd. Those filled with reasonable fear started to leave, one after another.

The old roach exhorted the crowd with determination. "Don't act like cowards, brothers. If we don't die like martyrs, we'll die like food for the queen. We need freedom. If we fight and die before we taste the sugar of freedom, our offspring will enjoy it. We'll be remembered because we spared them from being the food of your fat, lazy, greedy self-proclaimed queen." He turned his back on the mob. "I gotta go. I can do it alone if that's my fate. Those who feel they are roach enough can join me."

The old roach walked toward the palace. Behind him followed a dozen of the bravest roaches. Fear controlled the less brave of the crowd. They coldly dispersed, running for their lives.

At the palace's gate, the old roach led the small group of rebels in a surprise attack and won the first battle. The rebels broke into the palace, but the queen's guards quickly surrounded them. They retreated after heavy losses.

The queen was informed of the insurrection. She said quietly, with self-assurance, "Let them try, those rebels. They are just weak spots. They can't bring changes."

Almost the all territory joined and reinforced the "weak spots" led by the old roach. The rebels conquered the palace after suffering heavy losses. They bound together, lifted the queen on their backs, and threw her out of their territory.

Freedom was finally restored forever in the roaches' territory, courtesy of small and weak spots that united and moved stuff around.

Moral: Small and weak spots, when united, can become heavy vehicles able to move stuffs.

CHAPTER 31

THE DOG AND THE GUINEA PIG

A DOG WAS a great worker, always hunting for his food. He saved the extra food in his barn. However, whenever he left his house for his hunting adventures, a thief came in the barnyard and mercilessly stole the provisions that the dog had so dearly won.

The dog offered to hire his best friend, the guinea pig, to watch over his barnyard.

The guinea pig was a great choice because spying was his dream job. He accepted the offer as an honor. He found a hidden spot where he could observe the dog's barnyard from a distance.

As soon as the dog left for his work, the thief came.

"I saw the thief," the guinea pig reported excitedly when his boss came home. "It was the lazy, fat cat of the neighborhood. He stayed all day long, gnawing your supply. He just left when he heard your steps approaching. He went toward the river. I'm sure that if you run fast enough, you'll catch him."

The news infuriated the dog. He dropped everything he carried and ran as fast as he could toward the river. He saw the cat in the water, hiding. He furiously dived into the river but failed to catch the cat. He got out and waited for the disrupted water to calm. He could see the image of the cat in the water but was unable to catch the cat after many attempts.

The guinea pig, after following the dog slowly, asked him to relax. He pointed a finger up to show the dog where the cat was located. However, the dog kept looking at the guinea pig's finger instead of looking far, in the direction the finger was pointing.

In fact, the cat was perched in a tree by the river, and his image was reflected in the water. The guinea pig tried to show the dog where the cat was truly located, not in the water. But the dog failed to catch the guinea pig's message and consequentially failed to catch his robber.

Moral: When searching for something, relax and look again in every direction; the "thing" or the cause you are looking for may be in another direction. Sometimes, illusion, bias, and prototypes, to name that a few, may divert us from the true cause of something… A wise man, when showed a finger, looks in the direction it is showing, not at the finger itself.

CHAPTER 32

THE HEN AND THE TERMITES

WHILE SEARCHING FOR food for her chicks, a mother hen saw a termite mound from a distance.

"Perfect dinner spot for today and for many others to come," she thought. "But I've gotta use a strategy to get those termites out of their dormitory."

She found a perfect hiding spot for her baby chicks and walked alone toward the mound.

"Hey, guys!" she announced with a humble voice she had mastered after listening to a priest. "I'm a messenger from God. I've got good news from he who lives in heaven. He told me to tell every being that heaven on earth has just started. It's an everlasting life, imperatively free from starvations, wars, and atrocities. No one will ever need food, and predators will lie side by side with prey. They will also walk hand in hand as great friends. So come out and enjoy the new world order."

A massive laughter erupted from inside the mound, shaking even the ground around it.

The hen took a deep breath, feeling comforted. She thought her appeal was accepted with no resistance and with great acclamations. However, she realized that she had deceived herself when one of the termites answered her.

"You chickens are really very funny," the termite speaker pointed out wryly, **slighting** her with laughter. "You think you can dupe us again the same way your sister fooled us yesterday? We've heard that insane courting before. So, why don't you come up with something new? We got smart already!"

The hen, not impressed at all and not willing to give up, insisted, "I'm really sent by God. You can send one of you, a spy, out here to witness and verify my credentials. Really, God has started a new way of life out here. Come out and enjoy, please."

The termite speaker answered, "If I were you, I'd go back home and check my kids. You've been wasting your time here with a fake message while forgetting your main duty to protect your chicks." He looked upward. "All of them have been taken, one by one, by the hawk."

Looking above her, the hen saw a hawk effectively taking away one of her babies. She went back to the place she did hide them, but none were left. The raptor stole all of them. The hen wept desolately.

Moral: When attempting to play the smarter or the stronger, remember that there are always those who are smarter or much stronger than you—those who can do to you the same thing that you are trying to do to another.

CHAPTER 33

THE LEOPARD AND THE CHEETAH

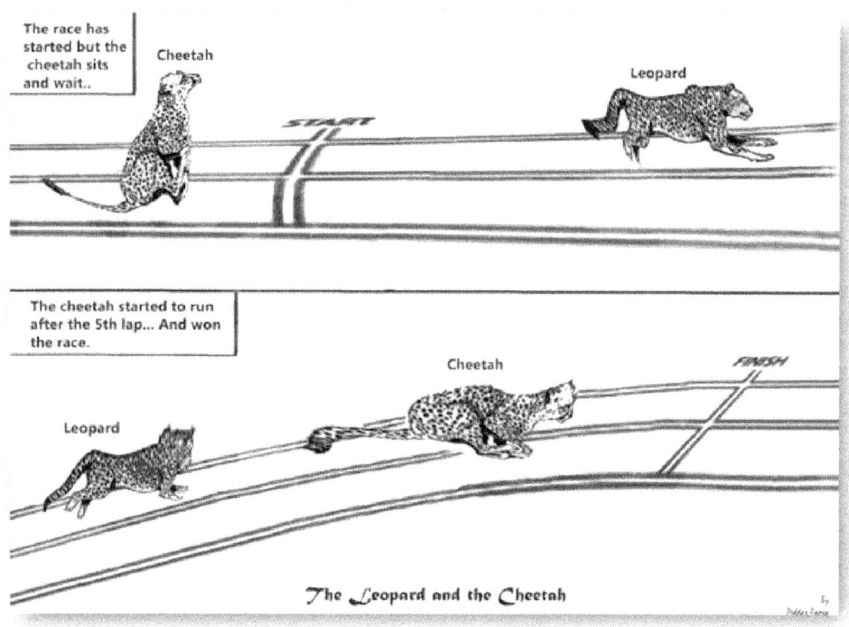

The race has started but the cheetah sits and wait..

Cheetah

Leopard

START

The cheetah started to run after the 5th lap... And won the race.

Cheetah

FINISH

Leopard

The Leopard and the Cheetah

A FAST LEOPARD, fooled by his grandiose and successful chases and captures of most of the fastest prey in the jungle, believed he could defeat a cheetah. He defiantly challenged him to a public race.

The cheetah accepted the challenge but warned the leopard, "I run faster than the roadrunner—even faster than the rhino. Why don't you challenge them first before you try to defeat me in a race?"

The leopard minimized those warnings and replied confidently, "I'm the best runner in the jungle. I'm the fastest runner you'll ever meet. If you believe that you're the best, to be the best, I gotta beat the best."

The race, considered by everyone in the jungle to be the race of a lifetime, took place in the jungle's stadium. The leopard received the support of almost all the jungle because the cheetah was a visitor; he didn't belong in the jungle.

At the starting point, after referees blew the departing whistle, the leopard started the race alone while the cheetah requested a seat to watch him run.

"Are you withdrawing or what?" inquired one of the referees.

"I'm not," the cheetah simpered. "Just watch the finish line."

"Is that because you think that your adversary is not at your level?" asked another referee.

"Just watch the finish line, please," the cheetah insisted with a deep composure.

The race was scheduled for six laps. When officials announced the fourth lap for the leopard, the cheetah stood up, ran as fast as he could, and won the race, to the extreme astonishment of the entire stadium.

Moral: Before you can think about defeating a "giant," challenge first those who are less powerful than he is.

CHAPTER 34

THE LION AND THE ZEBRA

THE KING OF the jungle, the almighty lion, was trapped in a hunter's snare. The more he struggled to release himself, the stronger the trap became. When he was exhausted and bleeding all over, he finally gave up and waited for his final hour to come.

He heard the sounds of footsteps approaching. "That's it!" he thought desperately. "I come to thee, Lord." The prayer continued in the form of a blessing to his son. "Just help my begotten son reign as wisely as he can—to be a better king than I was." He closed his eyes, courageously waiting for the hunter to finish him up with an arrow.

Nothing happened, and the sounds of footsteps were now moving away. He saw an innocent young zebra walking by. The lion begged for help.

After a long hesitation, the teen zebra took pity on the bleeding and almost-dying lion. Despite her fear, she decided to free him at her own risk because she knew that the lion, once freed, could turn against her and use her as food. However, the lion gave her his word not to devour her. "I'm too weak to attack you," the lion reassured her. "I've lost more than fifty percent of my blood. Please help me."

The teen zebra not only freed the almighty lion, she also helped him get back to his den. There, all the king lion's family not only paid their respects to her, but they also offered to let her marry His Highness, the prince lion, and have a share of the kingdom.

The zebra naively accepted the offers and became the third most powerful personality of the jungle with powers to give orders. She soon granted the zebra family immunity from any predator.

The mother of the newlywed princess was extensively opposed to her daughter's blind adventures. With the voice of experience, she advised, "There can't be such a marriage between a predator and his prey." She hit her hoof on the floor. "No matter what promise they made, they will end up consuming you up. No matter what power they gave you, it will just be temporary and really short-lived."

"What can I do, Mama?" retorted Princess Zebra with a childish voice openly exposing her innocence. "I've saved the lives of thousands of zebra in this kingdom. The prince loves me a lot. He's so grateful that I saved the life of His Majesty, the king lion. I don't believe that he will ever turn his back on me."

"I'll tell you what you need to get your divorce," contended the mother in an undertone. "Just cook only vegetables for your husband. Since he is a carnivore, he will divorce you quickly. In addition, you will come back to us, saving your life. We can't afford losing you."

Princess Zebra was bound by tradition to cook for her husband. After her conversation with her mother, she only served vegetables to the table for her husband as her mother recommended.

Prince Lion Junior acknowledged his wife's cooking change. "You were really made for me!" praised the hubby. "How did you guess that I was contemplating becoming a vegetarian? *Coup de chapeau!*"

Princess Zebra reported to mother, "It didn't work."

"Stop cooking for him," advised her mother forcibly. "He will divorce you quickly."

"If he gets hungry, Mama," said Princess Zebra, "isn't he gonna eat me?"

"Hell no. He'll only divorce you. No one in his family is going to allow him to eat you as long as his father, King Lion, is alive. But I'm afraid that he may change his mind and eat you after the death of the king. So, the faster we act, the more chance to save you we get."

On the third night, when no food was served to him, Prince Lion said appreciatively, "I love you, wife! I'm impressed that you knew that I was fasting in order to get closer to God. You are able to read my mind. That means that you are really mine."

His Highness, the prince, in recognition of the zebra's great act of saving his father, overcame all stratagems and misconducts the princess's mother suggested. Said act outweighed all negativity from Her Highness, Princess Zebra. Mother Zebra finally gave up. The lion and zebra couple lived happy regardless of their differences.

Moral: Love outweighs any wrongdoing. When you truly love your partner, like the prince lion loved Princess Zebra, you will easily forgive his/her misconduct. Also, love is stronger and greater than any limitation. It can help enemies—even "predators" and "prey"—live together beyond natural settings. Finally, a simple act of kindness, like that of the zebra to the lion, can be a fruitful key to your happiness—if the receptor is truly grateful.

CHAPTER 35

THE FARMER AND AN ANGEL

The Farmer and an Angel

A FARMER GOT lazy. Instead of plowing his field, he asked God to give him his daily bread. Surprisingly to him, God granted him his request and filled his barnyard with food. He enjoyed the free food for the entire summer and thanked God for his kindness.

After a short while, the farmer reasoned that God might not replenish his barnyard a second time. He put his fate back into his hands. He plowed his field tirelessly and grew crops that he estimated could last at least three years. Once again, the farmer thanked God for the blessings and the strength allotted to him for his accomplishments.

Unfortunately for him, a herd of elephants got in his farm and ate a large portion of his crop.

"Oh Lord!" the farmer complained sadly to God. "Why have you forsaken me? Why did you let those elephants wipe out the fruit of my labor? You know I don't have insurance."

"The manna I gave you," answered an angel sent by God, "was destined for the elephants. I gave it to you as a loan because you prayed for it. At the same time, elephants starved while you enjoyed their food. Now they deserve to eat your crop as your repayment."

"Oh my God!" the farmer protested vehemently. "Why didn't you warn me?"

"I said clearly," explained the angel, "that a man will eat from the sweat of his face. You ate your bread before you broke a sweat—it was a backward move, but it still satisfied the principle."

The farmer cried miserably.

Moral: What appears to be free may not be free at all.

CHAPTER 36

THE PYTHON AND THE BOA

A YOUNG AND small python was watching in amazement as a large boa swallowed a deer for his dinner.

The python was blown away after witnessing the successful completion of the boa's task.

"How did you do that?" the python asked the boa, who was about to take a long sleep. "You swallowed a prey much bigger than yourself."

"I've got talent!" the big snake replied nonchalantly and then asked the python to leave him alone because his resting time was ticking.

The python left him alone but said to himself, "Besides his size and age, the boa looks like me. If he can swallow a prey fifty times larger than his mouth, I can do it, too."

The python went on a hunting spree. Chance smiled on him quickly. He met a sheep that he quickly transformed into a dinner. In a blind effort to emulate the exploit of the boa, he directly engaged himself in a swallowing experience.

After successfully swallowing the sheep's head, the python could not swallow the sheep any farther. His mouth could not stretch enough to cover the rest of the sheep's body. Should he throw up or continue to swallow the sheep?

The sheep was stuck in his throat, and the python's struggle to get rid of the sheep increased his misery. He failed to throw it up, and the python suffocated.

Moral: Avoid to let the talents of your neighbor mislead you. In essence, all humans are said to be born equals, but they master things differently. Some are gifted and talented, yet others are just not as powerful as their peers.

CHAPTER 37

THE LION AND THE CHEETAHS

The Lion and the Cheetahs

FOUR BRAVE CHEETAHS plotted to challenge a mighty lion who kept crossing into their territory and disrupting their water. They climbed a tree by their pond and agreed to teach the stubborn and defiant lion a lesson.

"When that fat lion gets here," suggested one of the cheetahs, the oldest, smoking a cigarette, "we're all gonna jump at him on the count of three." He paused to evaluate his friends' opinions. "OK, everybody?"

"Yes, sir!" the band loudly and enthusiastically answered in unison like soldiers after receiving orders from their commander. They even saluted and took a military attention posture to accompany their acceptance.

In no time at all, the powerful lion crossed their turf. He looked stiffer, more intimidating, and fully aware of his indomitable might.

"There he is!" the older cheetah exclaimed enthusiastically, dropping the butt of the cigarette he was smoking. "Let him get closer to the pond, then…don't forget…don't forget, on the count of three, we gotta teach him a lesson."

The lion approached the water and disrupted it as always.

On the count of three, only three cheetahs jumped on the mighty lion. The eldest cheetah didn't join them.

They successfully, but not easily, chased the lion away from their territory, after, of course, incurring a lot of damages in term of bruises, wounds, some broken bones, and more.

After their legendary triumph, the three victorious heroes joined the old cheetah who didn't fight.

"I thought you said," said one of them, still rubbing his hurt neck and complaining of terrible pain, to the old cheetah, "that on the count of three, we were gonna jump on the poor lion. What went wrong?"

"The way you were screaming and working on him," the old cheetah clarified persuasively, lighting a cigarette, "assured me that you were getting it. I played the reserve force in order to counterattack the lion if he happened to be winning." He took a drag of his cigarette, and then he added with a husky voice and a forced smile, "Congratulations, guys, on your victory!"

The idea to fight the lion came originally from the old cheetah. However, he sincerely felt that he was too old to fight. What he had to do was just stimulate and encourage those younger than him to do the job.

The three cheetahs looked silently at one another. No comment was necessary. They knew that if it were not for their elder's choice to fight the lion, the latter would have been coming, unchallenged, to disrupt their water forever. The lion never came back.

Moral: Even though we may not be able to participate physically in an effort, our attitude and knowledge may stimulate others. Our wisdom may incite others to dream more, to decide better, or to act courageously.

CHAPTER 38

THE DOG AND THE DONKEY

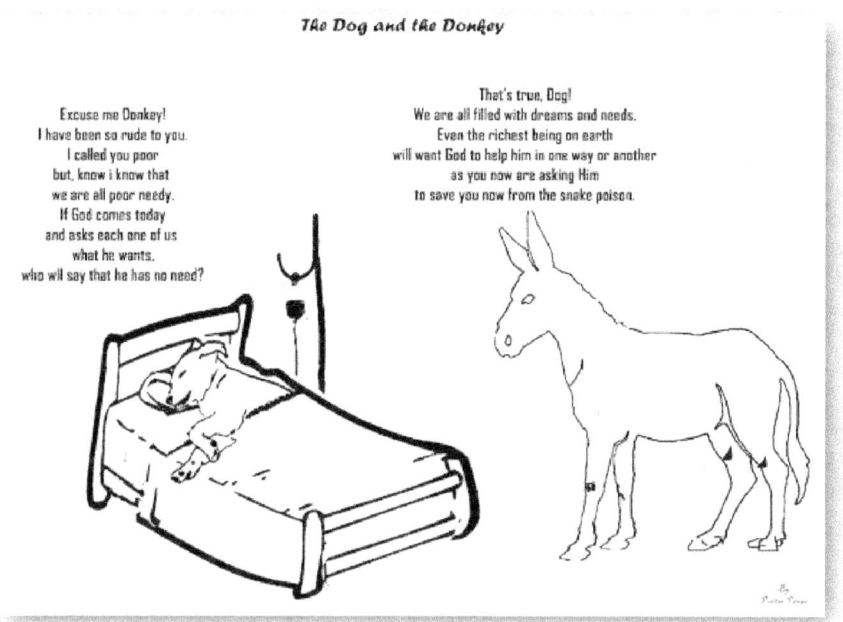

The Dog and the Donkey

Excuse me Donkey!
I have been so rude to you.
I called you poor
but, know i know that
we are all poor needy.
If God comes today
and asks each one of us
what he wants,
who will say that he has no need?

That's true, Dog!
We are all filled with dreams and needs.
Even the richest being on earth
will want God to help him in one way or another
as you now are asking Him
to save you now from the snake poison.

A HUMBLE DONKEY was dutifully carrying his master's loads to and from the farm every day.

A provoking dog used to laugh at him each time the donkey crossed by the dog's village. "See this slave and poor donkey!" barked the dog mockingly. "Always carrying a load that is not even his."

The donkey ignored the dog's comments. He did not regret his duty, nor did he care about the dog's opinion.

One particular day, the ever-present dog missed his daily criticisms. The donkey wondered why.

On his way back from the farm, he asked the villagers, "Where is the effervescent dog who always gives me hard time each time that I cross this village?"

"He was bitten by a poisonous snake," answered one of the villagers. "He's very sick and may be dying soon."

The donkey stopped to pay a visit to the sick dog. He found him storming heaven to save his life.

The donkey had compassion for him but could not do anything to save him.

"Here is a guy," thought the donkey, "who spent his life laughing at my nature and my conditions, calling me poor. Why is he praying now?"

"Pardon me, donkey!" said the dying dog, as if he had read the donkey's mind. "I was rude to you. I called you poor. But I know that everybody has a problem, in one degree or another. Now I know that nobody is rich, regardless of how much he is worth or how rich he thinks he is. We are all poor and needy. If today God comes and asks each one of us to openly tell him what he needs, who will say that he has everything and doesn't need God's help?" He sighed. "We are all needy!"

Moral: Everyone has needs and problems. There is no need to laugh at others' fates or misfortunes.

CHAPTER 39

THE DOG AND AN ANGEL

A DOG KEPT praying to have God tell him what to do. He wanted God to lead his life in order to avoid trouble with himself or with his community.

One day, an angel from God appeared to him. "God has granted your prayers," said the angel with compassion. "He says that he is going to guide you out of temptations, starting today."

The dog thanked the angel and got ready for his day. He had to go to a local stadium where his son was competing in a dog show. He was confident that God would lead him out of temptation and trouble.

During the event, in the fever of excitement, the dog talked so much that he offended those around him. A snack vendor crossed in from of him wearing a T-shirt with a logo that said, "I don't like your talk! Talk! Talk!" But the dog didn't pay attention. Finally, his talking upset another spectator, who jumped on him for a fight.

After his woe at the stadium, the dog was walking back home, wondering, "Why didn't God lead me out of the fight?" He shook his head in disappointment, but said, "God, may your will be done, but please, show me a good road that I can take to get home safely."

As he walked, the dog came to a junction. He didn't know which way to go. Coming from the road on the left, a swine wearing a T-shirt with a logo saying This Way, walked in from of him. But the dog paid no attention to the swine and took the road to the right. There, he met with a gang of loose dogs that beat the hell out of him.

Back home, the dog complained to God. "Why did you lead me into trouble today?"

"I did warn you, but you ignored me," answered the angel of God.

"No way!" protested the dog boldly. "I didn't receive any warning whatsoever from you. None."

The angel calmly reminded him about the vendor in the stadium and about the pig at the road junction. The dog's memory flashed back to him: "I don't like your talk…" Moreover, "This way."

He concluded that he had nobody to blame about that day's misfortune but himself. God, in fact, had warned and directed him, but he was too busy to pay attention and listen. He realized that God always guides, but it was up to him to be aware of his guidance.

Moral: Pay attention to your surroundings as they may contain clues for better choices and better direction of your daily affairs.

CHAPTER 40

King Gorilla and the Jackal

King Gorilla and the Jackal

IN THE ANIMAL kingdom, a gorilla reigned as a successful monarch. His subjects loved and respected him, and during his reign they enjoyed an unprecedented prosperity.

But flies were the scourge to his territory. There were more of them than the kingdom could handle. They caused epidemics and calamities, including many deaths among his subjects.

"I'm ordering you to kill every single fly," decreed the monarch. "Flies are terrorists, and they act against our well-being and security. Use any means necessary to exterminate them."

His subjects made a tireless effort to incapacitate the flies to keep them from doing further harm.

One day, while King Gorilla was resting, a jackal that worked in the palace saw a fly resting on top of the monarch's head. He picked up a wooden stick and hit the king's head very hard in order to kill the fly.

The fly effectively died, but in the process, the king gorilla was severely injured.

Royal guards arrested the jackal.

"You attempted to kill His Majesty," the chief of security accused him.

"No!" the jackal argued. "His Majesty ordained us to use any means necessary to kill flies among us. That's what I did."

King Gorilla acquitted the jackal but learned that any order decreed by authorities would affect the lives of millions, in one way or another, including themselves.

Moral: Authorities are not exempt from the consequences of their own decrees.

CHAPTER 41

THE TIGER AND THE MONKEY

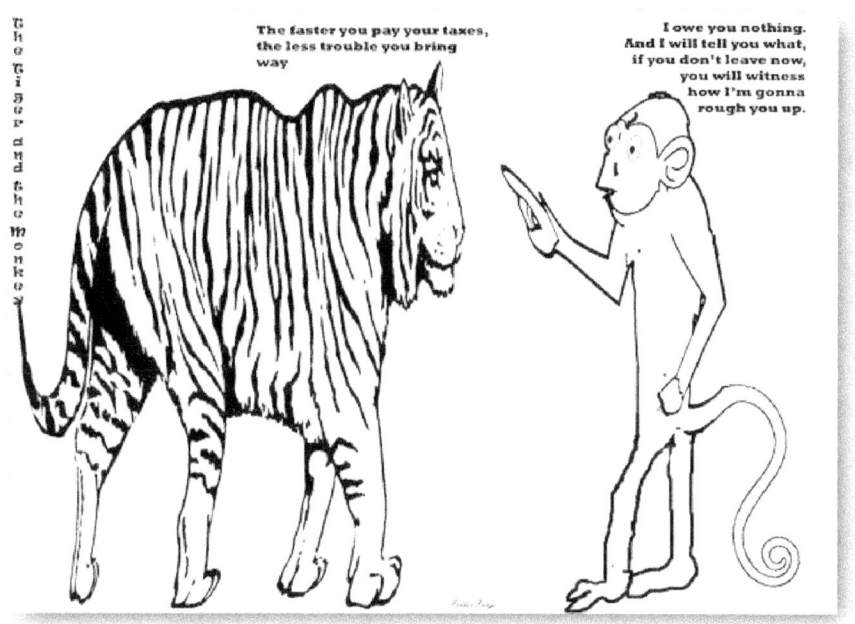

A TIGER INVADED a region populated by monkeys. He bullied them and imposed all kinds of rules on them, including taxes.

"The faster you pay your taxes," insisted the tiger, "the less trouble you'll bring to your community."

The tiger made daily tour of the monkeys' country to collect their dues and taxes. The governor did his best to avoid the furor of the tiger and collected all his requirements in due time.

One day, the tiger came by but didn't receive his self-proclaimed rights. He called a meeting. "Where are my taxes?" he furiously demanded. "I

99

give you ten minutes to bring me what you owe me. Otherwise, it's gonna be hell out here."

The chief of the territory stood against the tiger. "We owe you nothing," he said courageously. "You better leave our country now, or you will witness how I'm gonna rough you up."

The tiger hesitated. He could not believe his ears. The defying monkey was not even one percent as strong as he was. However, he was there, telling him to leave.

The defying monkey was seriously scared because he knew that his courage would cost him his life, but he did his best to conceal his fear.

A short silence followed, during which the tiger tried to decide whether to attack what he called the wretch monkey or retreat. He knew that the monkey was weak, but for him to get to that level of defiance, something must be going on.

"However," the tiger continued to deliberate mentally, "if this dumb monkey defeats me, that will be the end of all tigers. The news will spread all over the world. That will mean that no animal will ever fear us tigers anymore."

The tiger folded his tail and coldly retreated.

All the territory was reclaimed. The hero monkey was praised, and the victory was celebrated.

Morals:

1) Face your "giants." Whether they wear a face of fear, addiction, bullies, weakness, etc., those are mainly your own creation and they control you because you allow them to do so. The first step to take is to say no, then, with the time, if not immediately, the "giants" will pack they tool of domination, as well as recoil their tails, and leave you alone.
2) Courage pays.

CHAPTER 42

THE FROG AND THE LIZARD

A FROG AND a lizard were great friends. The lizard was older than the frog and was believed to have more knowledge than his friend. Most of the time, the lizard would instruct his friend to do this or that in a certain fashion or to just avoid this and that in order to protect himself and live longer.

The frog trusted him and followed his instructions to the extreme.

One day, the lizard told his friend to avoid eating crickets because, "They will make you sick."

The frog obeyed.

101

For a long while, the frog avoided eating crickets even when he wanted them the most.

A while after, the frog found the lizard eating crickets.

"Don't eat those crickets," the frog demanded. "You will get sick."

"Not anymore," the lizard replied calmly. "Things have changed. Crickets were temporary poisonous, but anymore."

The frog would not believe him and kept his diet—there would be no crickets on his menu.

That was how it went with the frog. He thought the lizard's advice was unchangeable, and he still liked to keep things the way they were back in the time.

The lizard tried to explain to him that every instruction or rule may work within a certain time frame or space. Even though there are unchanged, eternal rules, they have to be adapted to the period and space. Old ways should be regarded with new eyes.

Moral: Flexibility and adjustments are the keys to success.

CHAPTER 43

THE HAWK AND THE GUINEA FOWL

A HAWK PITILESSLY abducted the only child of a guinea fowl.

"Please, Master!" Madam Guinea Fowl pleaded remorsefully. "Let my son live, please. Take me instead."

The thief hawk ignored her heartbreaking supplications, leaving her in a deep state of desolation.

Later, while searching for her food, the guinea fowl heard a loud and continuous SOS. She followed the direction of the scream.

The guinea fowl was surprised to find that the same hawk that kidnapped her son days before was now trapped in a snare.

"Is that you?" questioned Madam Guinea Fowl, searching around for anything to hit the hawk with, but finding nothing. "I gotta finish you up. I must avenge my son."

"Don't hurt me, please!" the hawk implored pitifully, begging. "Save me, instead, please!"

"I think you forgot about me, don't you?" said Madam Guinea Fowl, full of rage. "Don't you remember forcing my son to be your lunch? The same prayer you are saying now, I said it to you then. But you ignored me. Why shouldn't I return the 'favor' you did for my son?" She made air quotation marks with her fingers when she pronounced the word *favor*.

"There is a reason you should let me live, ma'am!"

"Which is?"

"I swear that your son is alive," the hawk said convincingly. "Save my life in exchange for your son's freedom."

The guinea fowl's eyes opened wide in surprise. She had no time to assess the veracity of the hawk's statement. The sole mention of her son still being alive lit sparks of love in her heart. Her son meant the world to her. She missed him a lot and could not wait to see him again.

She freed the hawk. Nevertheless, the latter repaid her kindness by making her his dinner.

"That's how you thank me for saving your life?" asked the guinea fowl, attacked, wounded, and ready to be eaten.

"You must be a fool, stupid lady!" the hawk insulted her. "How could you believe such a pure lie? I didn't keep your son. I ate him after I took him from you. No predator can keep its prey alive. An enemy is an enemy forever. If you fail to defeat him, he will defeat you. Give him a chance and he will conquer you. No prey can save a predator, no matter the motive. It's like throwing yourself into a fire. It's an act of folly. It's suicide."

Moral: Stay away from people who bring trouble to you.

THE BAT AND THE BUFFALO

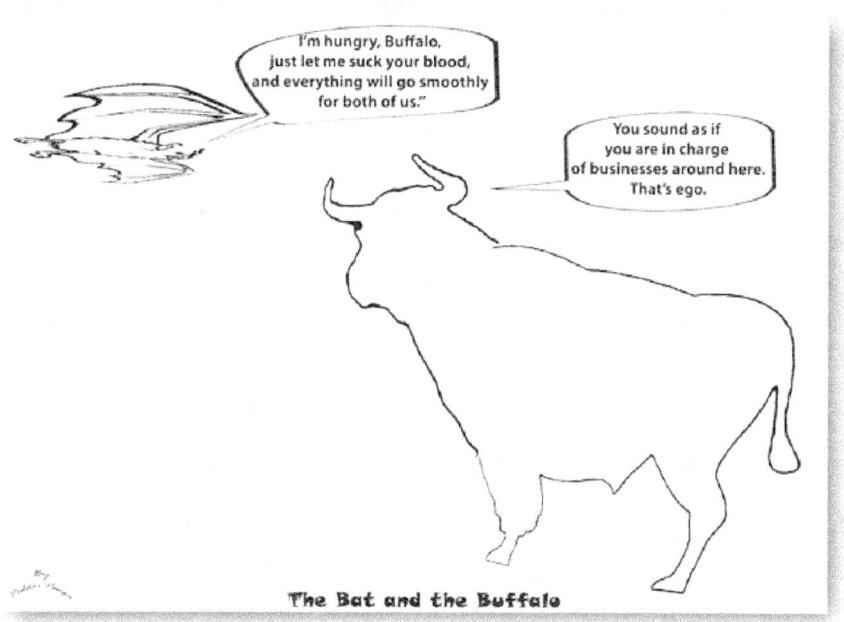

The Bat and the Buffalo

A HUNGRY BAT came near a buffalo, asking him for food.

"I'm so hungry, friend!" said the bat, as if he had a good reason. "Just give me your blood, and everything will go smoothly for both of us."

"Are you crazy or what?" riposted the buffalo, impressed. "Me, give you my blood? You gotta be dreaming. Wake up!"

"Listen, friend!" asserted the bat, using a persuasive tone. "I'm using wisdom I learned in observing a mosquito. Before it bites, it warns its targeted victim by singing in his ears."

"So you are trying to tell me that you came to warn me that I'm your targeted victim?" asked the buffalo. He realized that the bat's boldness wasn't impressive; it was troubling. "That's ego.

"That's not ego," the bat objected calmly, sounding more syrupy. "It's called help. I'm trying to help you if you help me suck your blood."

Master Buffalo made an effort to stifle a scornful smile. He thought it was one of the weirdest requests he had ever heard in his life. "Tell me a good reason why I should believe that you don't suffer from delusions of grandeur."

"If I bite you now," the bat explained tranquilly, "no other bat will ever bite you again. You'll be immune from other attacks. I don't have rabies. Other bats have it. And I will save you."

Master Buffalo stayed quiet for several seconds. The idea of having immunity against any future bat's bite and the immunity against rabies convinced him to allow the bat to bite him and suck his blood.

Hours or days passed before the buffalo felt sick from rabies. The bat had rabies and infected him with it.

"I shouldn't have listened to that bat at all," reasoned Master Buffalo, already disillusioned. "He took advantage of my listening ear."

Moral: A bully, a swindler, a flatterer, or anybody looking for his personal benefit to your detriment will succeed only if you listen to him.

CHAPTER 45

THE HENS AND THE FARMER

A ONE-EYED, BLIND farmer was drying a small portion of his seeds, which he spread on a carpet on the ground.

Because of the many birds circulating on his farm, including his own hens and other livestock, he decided to be on guard to protect his seeds. He placed a chair very close to the carpet and sat down, holding a long stick to chase birds away.

In the course of his guardianship, he felt a little bit sleepy and dozed off for a good while. During his drowsiness, he felt as if he were both awake and asleep at the same time. He could hear what the birds were saying.

"He is asleep!" said one hen to her peers. "Let's go peck carefully. Make sure we don't make noises."

"No, guys!" another hen said smartly. "The farmer is blind in one eye. To make it easier for all of us, let's go peck only on the portion of the carpet located on his left side, where his eye is blind."

The farmer awoke from his short nap, and after turning his head to his left, he effectively saw, with his right eye, many hens eating only the seeds on the portion of the carpet located on his left side.

The farmer was stupefied. He shook his head disbelievingly and said to himself, "Every being breathes the same air for a reason. Probably to help humans think better." He shook his head again. "Every being is important, or he would not have been created."

Before this event, the farmer was one of those who felt that humans were the only beings gifted with high intelligence and reasoning. All of God's other creatures were worthless and not intelligent at all.

Moral: Not only humans, but also animals, birds, and all beings have intelligence. They reason, they think, and they are wise. They are able to assess a situation and make good choices and good decisions depending on the circumstances offered to them.

CHAPTER 46

THE CAMEL AND THE MULE

A CAMEL AND a mule had been walking through a desert for hours, both carrying huge loads for their master.

The mule got tired. "Hey, friend!" he said to the camel. "I can't hold this load anymore. If I do, I may die. I'm really tired."

"Don't worry, mule!" replied the camel with compassion. "Just give me your entire load. I'll carry it for you."

The mule was so thankful for his relief and for his friend's help. However, his celebration was ephemeral because as they walked, the mule got weaker and weaker.

"I gotta tell you the truth, friend!" he announced to the camel after halting his progression. "I can't continue to walk anymore. I'm giving up."

"There is no need to," advised the camel encouragingly. "Just eat your food, drink plenty of water, and you'll feel revived."

"I have neither food nor water left. I finished my portion already."

"No problem," the camel encouraged him. "Take my portion of the food and water. Let's take a rest. Eat all my food, and then let's continue. We gotta be on time to deliver our loads; otherwise, trouble will visit us."

They took a short rest, during which the mule ate all of the camel's food and drank all his water.

They resumed their trip. But, after many hours, the mule had had enough.

"Here's the deal!" the mule said hopelessly, after stopping. "I'm now sick and broken beyond repair. I'm seriously tired, sleepy, hungry, thirsty, and weak. I can't continue to walk. Just leave me here. Dying will be a great relief for me."

"That's not an option!" the camel objected strongly. "I can't leave you behind. I can't let you die alone. I'm going to load you on my back. Get the rest you need, relax, enjoy the ride, and everything will be better for you."

The camel carried his friend and companion on his back with an open heart. That was in addition to his load and the mule's load. They made it safely to their destination.

The mule was so thankful that he loudly testified his friend's exploits to the entire village.

"Why did you do all of those favors for the mule?" asked one of the camel's peers.

"He is my friend," the camel commented joyfully. "A true friend must be there for better or worse."

"Do you think the mule would have done the same favor for you if you were in his situation?" asked another one of the camel's peers.

"Do you think he will ever return the favor in the future?" inquired another. "I believe that he will run away from you the same way the disciples ran away from Jesus when he was arrested."

"Guys!" the camel responded heartily. "I know that most friends and family members will leave you alone when you are facing crisis"—he shrugged—"but I helped the mule without expecting a reward or recognition."

Moral: When you are in trouble, the true friend is the one who stays, stands by your side, and helps you tirelessly, remorselessly, unrewardingly, and unconditionally.

CHAPTER 47

THE TURTLE AND THE SQUIRREL

MADAM TURTLE WAS a good friend to Lady Squirrel. They walked together, and every time there was a river or pond, the turtle carried the squirrel on her back to cross it by swimming.

"I can teach you to swim," Madam Turtle always said to her friend, "and how to take a bath."

"Water is made for drinking, not for bathing," the squirrel always answered.

The turtle knew that her friend, by her attitude against water, would never be able to swim.

One day, the squirrel had an emergency, but the turtle was not available to help her cross a river. She got stuck miserably on one side of the river while her son needed her on the other side.

The next day, the squirrel met her friend the turtle and asked her to teach her how to swim.

"You need to pay the tuition," said the turtle.

The amount seemed exorbitant for the squirrel. However, she had no other choice.

"OK!" the squirrel accepted. "But allow me enough time to gather your spoliating tuition, please."

After days, Lady Squired brought the fee needed for her swimming lesson.

"No, sorry!" the turtle categorically refused. "I only know how to swim; I don't know how to teach it. I'm sorry!"

"Why, then, did you ask me to bring you the tuition?" the squirrel asked fiercely, slavering with rage. "You made me waste my time and effort for nothing."

"My high tuition was another way of saying no," explained the turtle. "You should have understood my message. Besides, you should have learned to swim while you were amassing your tuition..."

"To learn to swim?" interjected the squirrel. "How could I? I was busy day and night amassing your tuition. When could I have learned to swim, and who could have taught me?"

Before Madam Turtle could answer, a lady goose came by to ask the turtle to teach her how to perfect her swimming performances and how to swim better in troubled waters and cross strong streams. The turtle accepted.

"You gotta be kidding!" remarked Lady Squirrel, deluded. "Now you know how to teach to a goose, but not me?" She took a very deep breath. "Why are you doing this to me, your best friend?"

"I will take you, too, as my student," approved the turtle with a broad smile.

The goose mastered her lesson in less than a week and graduated. But the squirrel, after couple of months, was still unable to perform the basic and first lesson of swimming.

Finally, they both gave up.

"Swimming is not made for me," the lady squirrel said regretfully, shaking her head. "I quit!"

"I knew that!" Madam Turtle said heartily. "That's why I refused to teach you in the first place, but you hollered like a wild human being." She hugged her. "You can't make wood with a banana tree."

Moral: No two beings are alike. Nature has bestowed particularities upon everybody. Every being is different in one way or another. Let nature have its way.

CHAPTER 48

THE DROWNING SKUNK

A FEMALE SKUNK wanted to cross a river. She failed to assess the force of the stream and blindly started to swim. In midstream, where the flow of the stream was great, she lost her equilibrium and could not swim anymore. She was carried downstream at a vertiginously high speed, and water filled her mouth as she struggled. She thought she was going to die.

However, chance smiled at her. She got stuck on a tree in the river. She started to scream loudly, calling for help.

"Help! Help! I need help. I'm drowning."

No one came. Those who were close by ran away because of the skunk's body odor. The skunk was so scared because, if the tree she was hanging on gave out, she would be done. Death was something she was not planning. So, she doubled and then tripled her screams and SOS calls.

"Help! Help! I need help. I'm drowning."

No response.

A few minutes later, the skunk looked around to evaluate her position. She was surprised to find that the tree she was preciously hanging on was located not far away from the shore. In addition, from there, the stream of the river was weak.

She reached the riverbank with very little effort.

"Oh my God." The skunk sighed, panting and holding her chest, relieved. "If only I'd have mastered my fear earlier and looked around, I could have saved myself from unnecessary struggle and from screaming for help that would never have come."

Moral: Fear is the number-one enemy of every being. Usually, there is little danger but a lot of fear. When faced with trouble, master your fear and look around. You may have a solution handy—a solution that may be laughing at you while it's waiting to be used.

A Rambling Cat

A CAT WAS rambling peacefully in a neighborhood, not knowing where to go or what to do.

He unfortunately stepped on a sharp nail by the road.

"Aie!" The cat grimaced in pain. "That really hurt!"

The nail got stuck deep in his paw. It took him extra effort coupled with great pain to remove the nail and to stop the bleeding.

The moment of agony passed. The cat was about to resume his walk, but he mumbled to himself, "I've got to put this nail back on the road so that anybody else who steps on it feels the pain I just felt."

With satisfaction, he planted the nail, tip up, on the road with the intent of passing his misfortune to the next victim.

He continued his hiking activity that he quickly transformed into a fitness exercise. He also quickly forgot about the nail and the distress it had caused him.

After a long while, the domestic feline decided to walk back home. Unfortunately, he stepped on the same nail that had hurt him earlier.

"Oh my God!" the cat screamed loudly and unpleasantly. "Why only me? I set up this nail to hurt others, but instead I hurt myself again."

This time the nail got deeper in his paw. He could feel the pain of the sting on his bone as well as deeper in his heart.

He pulled the nail from his paw with much more effort and extreme suffering than the first time. However, this time, he threw it away instead of planting it on the road again with the intent to hurt others.

"I got wise now," concluded the cat after he returned home. "I have to make good choices that will benefit me and my community. What I wish for myself is what I should wish for my neighbor."

Morals:

1) When a misfortune crosses your path, make sure you clean the disaster after you. If you wish your disaster to happen to somebody else, it may strike you again, maybe harder than the first time. Sometimes, penalties apply for recidivists.
2) Sometimes people learn better when something unusual happens to them. The "unusual" opens opportunities for improvements and for resetting the standards, including the habits and reasoning.

CHAPTER 50

THE RACCOON AND THE DOLPHIN

MISTER RACCOON WAS one of the carpenters of the jungle. He kept complaining about his duties because he was often injuring himself.

One particular day, while hitting a nail into a piece of wood, he smashed his finger with a hammer.

"Ouch," he complained. "I have to stop this carpeting job. It doesn't like me. I have encountered too many injuries, including falling from ladders and rooftops. I have hurt my back so many times already. I need to act now and abandon this work, or I may lose my life soon."

Back home, his wife didn't agree with him. She suggested that he consult with the dolphin, by the sea, who was reputed to be as wise as Solomon.

"You are not practicing your job with love," explained the wise dolphin to the raccoon. "Your work is just mechanical. You are filled with tension. Put a lot of love into your work, and you will see the difference." He paused. "Complaint is a younger brother to anger. Observe closely someone who is angry, and you will see how drained of love he looks. Love will bring attention and protection. Complaints are just another way of blocking the flow of love. The more you complain, the more love you sweep out of your heart, the more mechanical you become, and the more injuries you get."

"How can I act and lead my life with love?" asked the raccoon excitedly.

"Before starting your work, or anything that you do," answered the dolphin with a broad smile, "say and repeat to yourself that you are working or doing it with love, for love, and in the name of love. Then believe it. Don't unconsciously say it. Feel it." He cleared his throat. "After your work be thankful and be filled with gratitude even if it seems that things didn't work according to your expectations. Gratitude and love work hands in hands. The first helps the heart unfold to allow more waves of love to fill it. The more love you get filled, the more gratitude you give; and the more gratitude you give, the more love you get filled." He increased the degree of his smile to the extent that it contaminated his interlocutor. "This technique works for me, and I hope it's going to work for you, too," concluded the sea mammal.

"How if you forget to say to yourself that you have to act with love?" the raccoon inquired, worried but still under the contagious effect of the dolphin's broad smile.

"It's natural to forget, but the next time you remember, do as I told you and act as if you never forgot," the dolphin advised.

"Thanks a bunch," The raccoon appreciated the dolphin's advice.

Mister raccoon followed the advice of the wise dolphin and enjoyed many years of fruitful work. He came to realize for sure that love heals all wounds, love is the answer to every problem, and love make things easier.

Moral: Act with love and be grateful everywhere and every time in order to facilitate your life. Love is the way of life.

THE END

ABOUT THE AUTHOR

Peddar Y. Panga

AUTHOR PEDDAR PANGA was born in 1974 and raised in the Democratic Republic of Congo, Africa. He immigrated to the United States at age thirty. He graduated from Texas A&M University - San Antonio, with a bachelor of science in biology and a minor in psychology. He also attended San Antonio College, where he majored in drama, nursing, and general science.

Peddar enjoys doing interpretation works as a hobby. He speaks English, French, Portuguese, Spanish, Swahili, and many other African languages. He also loves acting, singing, traveling, and sports. He is a soccer and basketball referee. He also volunteers at different health-care facilities.

Letters and comments from readers are welcome! Please write at peddarpanga@gmail.com.

INDEX

breakfast, 41-42, 74
breath (ing), 2, 21, 42, 55, 80, 113
breeze, 23
brethren, 75
brother(s), 10, 19-20, 26, 47-48, 52, 56-57, 69-70, 74-75, 119
    killed his big, 40
buffalo, 105-106
bull, 72-73
bully (bullies), 100, 106
bunny, 1
bystander(s), 14

Cage, 4, 12
calamity (calamities), 32, 97
camel, 109-111
cancer, 72
candidate for your own distraction, 55
capable, 24
capacity (capacities), 56
carnivore(s), 2-3, 84
career, 31
carpenter(s), 118
carpet, 107-108
carrot, 60
cat, 77-78, 116-117
cause
    the true, 78
celebration, 109
challenge, 69-70, 81-82, 90
    of the century, 70
chance(s), 27, 65, 85, 89, 114, 104
    by, 16
    of success, 36

goal, 75,
goat(s), 40
God, 3, 9-10, 32, 52, 73, 79, 80, 85, 86-87, 94, 95-96, 106
    oh my, 87, 114, 117
golden,
    hand, 29
    opportunity, 11
Goliath, 70
gorilla, 97-98
grace, 10,
graciously, 29
grandeur, 106
grandfather, vii-viii
grandiose, 81
gratitude, 118-119
greediness, 42
guarantee,
    of success, 75
guard(s), 49-50, 76
    royal, 98
guardianship, 49, 107
guidance, 96
guinea fowl, 103-104
guinea pig, 77- 78

Habit(s), 41, 44, 47, 48, 117
    destructive, 55
    giving, 59
    natural, 48
habitat, 20
hammer, 10, 118,
hamster, 4-6,

www.ingramcontent.com/pod-product-compliance
Lightning Source LLC
Chambersburg PA
CBHW071254130626
46556CB00003B/1303